Falling

By

Falling

By Jade Winters

Published by Wicked Winters Books

Copyright © 2020 Jade Winters

www.jade-winters.com

All rights reserved. This book or any portion thereof may not be reproduced or used in any manner whatsoever without the express written permission of the author.

All characters in this publication are fictitious and any resemblance to real persons, living or dead, is purely coincidental.

ISBN: 979-8-632-23857-1

Other titles by Jade Winters

Novels

143
Caught by Love
Guilty Hearts
Say Something
Faking it
Second Thoughts
Secrets
In it Together
Love Interrupted
The Song, The Heart
Accidentally Together
Flirting with Danger
Unravelled
Lost in You
Starting Over Again
Just One Destiny
Picking the Right Heart
The Second Time
Looking for Ms Right
Torn
Always You
All That Matters

The Ashley McCoy Detective Series

A Walk into Darkness
Everything to Lose

Novellas

Talk Me Down From The Edge

Chapter One

Amelia stared woefully at her reflection in the mirror, her eyes awash with tears. *What's wrong with me? Am I really that bad?*

Despite having 'I am Enough' Post-it Notes plastered all over her bathroom mirror, Amelia felt far from enough. In fact, her self-worth couldn't have been any lower. She knew in her heart of hearts that she shouldn't need another person's desire to validate her, but it was so hard, especially when she'd been single for over a year. A year without love. Without sex. Was that a record? At her age, she should have been fighting women off, not sitting in her flat, waiting to see if yet another emotionally unavailable woman was going to dump her after their first date.

Amelia accepted it was a sign of the times – where men and women were a commodity. Dating apps had seen to this. She always likened the online dating process to searching for a job. You put all that effort into finding exactly the right fit for you and, after what you thought was an amazing interview, nothing. At least with a job application the company didn't ghost you if you contacted them afterwards. Amelia gave a bitter laugh at the thought of how many times this had happened in her personal life. Twenty-five dates later and none had gone further than a snog.

It wasn't as if Amelia hadn't been warned by her

friends that internet dating was not for her. It was a jungle out there, she'd been told right before putting her profile on Meet and Greet, but did she listen? No! She never did. Somehow, she had tried to convince herself that it would be different for her. That her potential soulmate would be able to see her true qualities, and together they would sail off into the sunset.

How quickly that dream dissolved into a pile of nothingness.

Why couldn't women just be honest about how they felt? The mind games they played messed with her head. So much so, that after today's latest let down, she had deleted her profile on the dating app and sworn herself to lifelong celibacy. *What I don't have, I won't miss.*

Hearing her mobile phone ring, Amelia pursed her lips and mentally prepared herself for the dialogue she had been practicing in her head all evening, on the off-chance Liz did actually call.

It was ten p.m. Their date was meant to have been at seven.

Dropping her voice an octave to give the impression she had just woken up, she said, 'Hello.'

'Hey! Sorry about the—'

'No need to apologise, Liz.' Pause. 'You actually did me a favour by not turning up tonight.'

'I did?'

Amelia could hear the slight hesitation in her voice.

'Yes. I've got an important meeting tomorrow, the last thing I needed was to be exhausted.'

'Eh? Why would you be exhausted?' Liz said. 'We were only going for a drink.'

'Believe me, Liz, we were going to be doing more than that. Much, much more,' Amelia said in her most sultry voice.

For the next five minutes, Amelia told Liz exactly what she had planned to do to her with the most graphic descriptions. She went into so much detail, she actually turned herself on. By the end of the fantasy scene Amelia had memorised from an erotica book earlier, she could almost hear Liz panting down the line.

'Well, I'd better go now—'

'No wait! Let me come over. I can be there in fifteen… no ten minutes.'

'Too late I'm afraid….'

'Come on—'

Amelia put her mouth to the phone and let out a soft, seductive sigh before disconnecting the call. Almost immediately the phone started to ring again. Without looking at the caller ID, she waited a few seconds. Liz was keen. Amelia was glad the technique had worked on her. Maybe she'd think twice about standing someone up in the future.

Swiping to accept the call, she frowned when a familiar voice that wasn't Liz spoke into her ear.

'Who's the bestest friend in the world?'

'Er… you,' Amelia said, hazarding a guess.

'Damn right I am.'

There were a few moments of silence before Cecile spoke again.

'Remember that trainee position you applied for at Styles?'

'Yeah, what about it?'

'Well, looks like you're in with a chance.' Cecile worked as an admin assistant at Styles so would be one of the first to know.

Amelia held the phone with a trembling hand. 'When I didn't hear back from them, I assumed they didn't want me.'

Cecile laughed. 'Only you could assume the worst from a lack of response.'

'Come on, just tell me what's happening?'

'They're starting the hiring process, and you've got an interview!'

'What? Are you bloody kidding me?'

'Nope, but you're up against some serious competition.'

Amelia's heart sank. *That's the story of my life.* 'Go on, who are they?'

'People from Pascha and Converts—'

'Pascha! Converts? Please tell me you're joking.'

'Do I sound like I'm joking? Anyway, thanks to your BFF shoving your portfolio under the nose of Damien in HR, you've got as good a chance as anyone. You'll officially hear from them tomorrow, but your interview's on Wednesday.'

Amelia struggled to take it all in. 'Wednesday? But that's only two days away. I haven't got anywhere to stay or—'

'You can stay with me. I thought you'd be happy.

Do you know what having Styles on your CV can do for your career?'

Amelia steadied herself using the basin for support. She was right. Where was her gratitude? *I've got an interview!! I've got an interview!! Oh my God! Oh my God!*

Eyes closed, she pinched herself, quickly suppressing the urge to scream 'Ouch' having pinched a little too hard.

'Are you still there?'

I think so. Amelia's eyes darted around her small bathroom, unsure where to settle her gaze. With a jolt, Amelia realized she hadn't responded.

'Oh, um yes, sorry, it's just um my… there was a spider on my head,' Amelia blurted out the first thing that came to mind and instantly regretted it.

'A spider on your head?'

'Er yeah, it um lives here.' *Please stop talking nonsense.* 'Anyway, sorry, Cecile, I can't thank you enough for helping me with this. And I'm grateful, I just can't believe it.'

Amelia could hear the immediate reprimand in Cecile's voice. 'I told you, you've got to believe in yourself. If you won't—'

'I know, I know, no one else will.'

'Right, you're not in your PJs?'

Amelia turned towards the mirror and took in her casual outfit. Jeans and a tight-fitted striped grey waistcoat. She would be the first to admit it wasn't over the top glam, but the look was stylish enough. For Bournemouth anyway. 'No, why?'

Amelia could hear laughter in the background.

'Cause we're coming to get you.'

'You're in Bournemouth?'

'Yes, I'm with the girls, we had free tickets to a fashion show earlier. Now we're ready to hit the town.'

'Oh right. You know, Cecile, it's kind of late and—'

'Oh, don't be such a bloody bore. You're the oldest twenty-eight-year-old person I know.'

Amelia shook her head incredulously. 'And you're the youngest thirty-year-old I know.'

'I'll take that as a compliment.' More laughter. 'Put your face on, we're five minutes away.'

And with that, the line went dead.

Amelia rolled her eyes. *Great.* Now she was going to be stuck in a straight club watching Cecile and her friends be ogled by pimple-faced teenagers. She'd had the misfortune of going out a few weeks back and was shocked that most of the 'men' looked no older than sixteen. She could think of nothing worse than spending another night in such a place.

Maybe I should call Liz back. Amelia's new-found confidence at being given a shot at her dream job had boosted her self-worth.

She started to punch in Liz's number then stopped. Amelia didn't need her. She didn't need anyone. That's what she loved about life. Just when you thought things couldn't get any worse, it flipped and did the total opposite.

A fleeting grin appeared on Amelia's face as she thought about all the attractive women she would meet in her new job. That's if she managed to impress the

Do you know what having Styles on your CV can do for your career?'

Amelia steadied herself using the basin for support. She was right. Where was her gratitude? *I've got an interview!! I've got an interview!! Oh my God! Oh my God!*

Eyes closed, she pinched herself, quickly suppressing the urge to scream 'Ouch' having pinched a little too hard.

'Are you still there?'

I think so. Amelia's eyes darted around her small bathroom, unsure where to settle her gaze. With a jolt, Amelia realized she hadn't responded.

'Oh, um yes, sorry, it's just um my… there was a spider on my head,' Amelia blurted out the first thing that came to mind and instantly regretted it.

'A spider on your head?'

'Er yeah, it um lives here.' *Please stop talking nonsense.* 'Anyway, sorry, Cecile, I can't thank you enough for helping me with this. And I'm grateful, I just can't believe it.'

Amelia could hear the immediate reprimand in Cecile's voice. 'I told you, you've got to believe in yourself. If you won't—'

'I know, I know, no one else will.'

'Right, you're not in your PJs?'

Amelia turned towards the mirror and took in her casual outfit. Jeans and a tight-fitted striped grey waistcoat. She would be the first to admit it wasn't over the top glam, but the look was stylish enough. For Bournemouth anyway. 'No, why?'

Amelia could hear laughter in the background.

'Cause we're coming to get you.'

'You're in Bournemouth?'

'Yes, I'm with the girls, we had free tickets to a fashion show earlier. Now we're ready to hit the town.'

'Oh right. You know, Cecile, it's kind of late and—'

'Oh, don't be such a bloody bore. You're the oldest twenty-eight-year-old person I know.'

Amelia shook her head incredulously. 'And you're the youngest thirty-year-old I know.'

'I'll take that as a compliment.' More laughter. 'Put your face on, we're five minutes away.'

And with that, the line went dead.

Amelia rolled her eyes. *Great.* Now she was going to be stuck in a straight club watching Cecile and her friends be ogled by pimple-faced teenagers. She'd had the misfortune of going out a few weeks back and was shocked that most of the 'men' looked no older than sixteen. She could think of nothing worse than spending another night in such a place.

Maybe I should call Liz back. Amelia's new-found confidence at being given a shot at her dream job had boosted her self-worth.

She started to punch in Liz's number then stopped. Amelia didn't need her. She didn't need anyone. That's what she loved about life. Just when you thought things couldn't get any worse, it flipped and did the total opposite.

A fleeting grin appeared on Amelia's face as she thought about all the attractive women she would meet in her new job. That's if she managed to impress the interviewer.

Finally, the lady downstairs might be getting some action.

Chapter Two

The next day, Amelia was packed and ready to go. After one last glance around her studio flat to make sure she'd not left any electrical items on, she stepped out into the communal hallway and closed the door behind her. If all went well with her interview, it was likely she'd have to give up her tenancy. There was no way she could commute between London and Bournemouth every day. Did she feel the slightest bit of sadness and regret at the prospect? No. It was moments like this that reminded Amelia why she didn't mind being single sometimes. Having no one to answer to meant she could take off at the drop of a hat without having to explain herself to anyone. She wasn't held back by emotional blackmail, or guilt for working away from home to earn a living.

As much as she would have loved a furry companion to go home to at night, they were too much responsibility. They needed feeding, vet visits and companionship, just to name a few, and she wasn't in the right space to provide any of those. Though Amelia had made a promise to herself that once she was financially solvent, she would have two cats, a dog and a rabbit. *And maybe a tortoise.*

Amelia pulled onto the M3, following the signpost to London. According to her Sat Nav, Islington – her final destination, was two hours and thirty minutes away. As she crawled behind the mounting traffic in front, she reached over to the glove compartment to retrieve a CD. Distracted for no more than a few seconds, she hadn't realised a car had stopped in front of her until it was too late.

The noise of the two cars making contact startled her more than the actual crash itself.

Thankfully, she'd only been crawling along at five mph.

Amelia edged her car onto the hard shoulder and the car in front did the same. The driver of the other car got out and walked around to the rear of her vehicle to inspect the damage.

Oh shit! By the scowl on the woman's face, it didn't look good. In her mind's eye, Amelia could just see the insurance policy landing on her door mat with an extortionate increase in her premiums.

The woman turned her attention to Amelia who was still sat in her car, her fingers tightly wound around the steering wheel. Her number one pet hate was confrontation, and the woman standing there waiting for her looked like she liked nothing but getting straight to the point.

Reluctantly, Amelia released her seatbelt, made a show of rotating her neck and slowly climbed out of the car.

'I'm—'

'Were you on your phone?' the woman asked accusingly.

Amelia frowned. 'What? No, of course not.'

The look the woman gave her told her that she

didn't believe her. 'I swear I wasn't—'

'Then you must have been asleep?'

'Look, I'm sorry. I was looking for something—'

'Looking for something on the motorway?' the woman said with a shake of her head.

'In my glove compartment.'

'Let me guess, you're from Bournemouth?'

'I am actually,' Amelia replied defensively. 'You got a problem with that?'

'No, what I've got a problem with is people who are so accustomed to driving in a town full of oldies, that they forget their senses when they come out into the real world.'

'Now hold on a second—'

'No, you hold on. You could've caused a lot of damage.'

'Hardly! I was barely moving.' Amelia fired back more out of frustration than anything else.

'Are you fucking kidding me? I've got valuable stuff in my boot.'

At this, Amelia felt a prickling sensation behind her eyes. Blinking away the tears, Amelia looked down at the ground.

When she spoke, her voice was choked with emotion. She hated people raising their voice to her. 'I'm sorry. I… if… if I've damaged anything….'

As hard as Amelia tried to keep her tears at bay, they wouldn't obey her, and slowly rolled down her cheeks. Using the back of her hand to wipe them away as she scurried back to her car, she reached inside and retrieved her mobile phone from her bag.

When she shut the car door, the woman appeared beside her. Her features no longer hard.

'I'm sorry if I was a bit harsh.'

A bit? Instead of making her feel better, the woman's kindness only made Amelia feel worse.

'There's no need for you to apologise,' Amelia said. 'I was in the wrong.'

'Yeah, but no damage was done this time. My stuff is okay, the car just has a small scratch. It's no biggie, let's just leave it.' The woman smiled and it transformed her whole face. 'Are you okay?'

Amelia nodded.

The woman's eyes slowly roamed down Amelia's body then back up again to her face.

'You're looking a bit pale. I've got some water in my car.' The woman gestured for Amelia to follow her and she slowly trailed behind.

The woman leant into her car and backed out holding a bottle of water which she handed to Amelia. 'When you get to where you're going, maybe it would be best to have a shot of brandy to put some colour back in your face.'

Amelia acknowledged the drink with a nod of thanks and took a mouthful. She hadn't realised how dry her throat was. She took another sip and attempted to give the water back to the woman.

'Keep it.'

'You sure?'

'Yes.' The woman looked at her watch and turned

to go. 'I'd better make a move. Please drive a bit more carefully.'

'Point taken,' Amelia said. 'And again, I really am sorry.'

The woman leant against her car and held Amelia's gaze, as if she was actually seeing her for the first time. The intensity of her stare caused Amelia's breath to catch in her throat. If the woman was waiting for her to say something, she was going to be in for a long wait. Amelia was suddenly speechless. She had been so caught up in her head contemplating what could have happened, that she hadn't realised how attractive the woman standing in front of her was. Did she say attractive? She meant hot! Top of the scale hotness.

Now is not the time to be checking out the woman whose car you just hit!

By the time Amelia finally found her voice, the woman had climbed into her car. The engine started and seconds later the car re-joined the traffic, with the woman waving out of the window, leaving Amelia standing there dumbstruck.

This might not have been the best start to the day, but Amelia was sure things could only get better.

Chapter Three

Melissa periodically checked her rear-view mirror until the figure she'd left behind diminished in size, before finally disappeared altogether. Despite her initial irritation at the stranger's clumsiness, she couldn't help but smile. For some reason, the woman had left a lasting impression on her, despite only being in her company for five minutes. *Five minutes?* It normally took weeks for a woman to do that. If at all.

It was a shame they hadn't met under more favourable circumstances. If she'd had more time on her hands, Melissa could have asked the stranger if she wanted to go for a coffee at a service station. Of course it would have been under the guise of calming her nerves, but the main objective would have been to get to know her better, much better. Melissa could still see her flushed cheeks. The slight tremble of her lips.

Melissa gave herself a quick reality check. *And I wonder why lesbians get the reputation of falling in love at first sight. Next, I'll be fantasising about us moving in together and raising babies.*

Right, forget about her, I need to focus. Melissa had a million and one things to do today, and she was already behind. If, for some reason, she fucked up, Vogue would be even more pissed off with her than she already was. 'Heads are gonna roll' was one of Vogue's favourite sayings, and Melissa knew she meant it, having been the recipient of that threat many times.

Changing lanes, Melissa ran through the mental check list in her mind. Shopping was done – two cases of Cristal champagne. Lobsters and caviar were still intact in iceboxes in the car boot. *Nothing but the best for the boss.*

Earlier that day, Melissa thought Vogue had been joking when she'd told Melissa to go and pick up the champagne and food from Dorset. But Melissa should have known better. Vogue's sense of humour wasn't that straightforward. She thought her own jokes were amusing but no one else's. *What a waste. Like there aren't more important things that need to be taken care of.*

But like the dutiful person she was, Melissa had done so without question. Like she always had throughout the time she had worked for Vogue.

Vogue was the leader and Melissa the follower.

Vogue always got the girl and Melissa always got the leftovers. The ones she didn't want or the ones she discarded. The ones who cried on Melissa's shoulder after Vogue had left them heartbroken.

Melissa hoped that once she removed herself from Vogue's shadow, all that would change. As long as she stayed, it would always be the same. It wasn't that Melissa wasn't attractive or didn't have charisma of her own. It was just when Vogue was around, Melissa became invisible. While Vogue played Ms. Charming, mesmerising her prey with her wit and captivating regal air, Melissa could only fade into the background and watch from afar. Yes, she was jealous, madly so, but she knew that one day the boot would be on the other foot.

She would be the one lapping up the attention and everything else she deserved.

Problem was that Melissa just didn't know when.

But she would have her day.

That, she was sure of.

Chapter Four

'Come on people, in my office now,' Vogue called out as she strode through the open-plan office area that led directly to a glass-walled conference room. Despite the dire circumstances, a small smile curved her lips as she pushed open the door. It always amused her the way her employees sat erect whenever she made her imposing entrance. Not that she wanted them to be afraid of her. No, but commanding respect was no small feat, especially from a bunch of talented people like most of them were. What it boiled down to was knowing that they needed a leader and Vogue was born to lead. She wasn't one of those indecisive people who couldn't tell their arse from their elbow.

First through the door was Lindsay, Styles Head of Marketing. Vogue looked upon her as a godsend. Bright, intelligent and as fiery as her wild red hair. The woman should have had 'Ambitious' tattooed on her forehead. Vogue had never known such a go –getter, apart from herself of course.

'Are you still going to that networking event tonight?' Lindsay asked.

Lindsay dropped onto a seat and placed her coffee straight onto the polished oval-shaped table.

At this, Vogue raised an eyebrow, a gesture that had Lindsay shoot her a sheepish smile as she moved her cup onto a coaster.

Vogue walked around the table placing a folder

before each of the eight seats. 'It's been cancelled. Anyway, there's no point networking if we don't have a new collection. We'll all be looking for a job.'

Vogue didn't let the thought linger too long in her mind. If the company went bust, she knew she would have to look for a job in another industry altogether. There was no way she would be able to survive the humiliation. It was bad enough she found herself in this position in the first place. Especially as the company being on its last legs was not her doing. Her so called best friend and business partner, Bev, had plagiarized their last collection from a college student, claiming they were her own designs and implied Vogue was in cahoots with her. The student threatened to go public, a move that would not only have ruined the company's reputation, but Vogue's name as well.

The substantial sum Vogue paid to avoid her reputation being tarred, was enough to bring Styles to its knees financially.

Bev had gone into hiding since the revelation, leaving Vogue to question why she had lied. It wasn't as if Bev didn't have the capability to produce amazing work, because she could. She had been doing it for years. So to say this latest episode had hit Vogue like a tonne of bricks was an understatement. If only she knew why Bev had felt the need to betray her, she could at least try and make sense of things. But nothing had been forthcoming from Bev. A woman who Vogue had loved like a sister. A woman who had shit on her from a great height!

Thankfully, Tina, an old friend, had thrown her a lifeline days before she was considering shutting the doors on Styles for good. If Vogue could come up with a new collection, Tina had promised to get her designs on the major catwalk shows, giving her exposure to buyers from department stores worldwide.

Vogue had learnt a valuable lesson while she'd been holed up at home, licking her wounds. That if she was going to come back bigger and stronger, she needed to move her company in a new direction. It was no longer financially viable to design clothes exclusively for wealthy women who would only wear the garments once or twice, then bury them in the back of their wardrobe.

As people often kept the same coats and jackets for years, what Vogue now envisioned was an outwear collection which would carry the mark of her unmistakable brand badge on the sleeve.

Not one to look a gift horse in the mouth, Vogue had arranged a meeting with the bank to take out a much-needed loan. This was necessary to pay for the whole slew of new and forward-thinking designers she had lined up to make magic happen. But now, with the company funds so low, even a loan wouldn't be enough, and she was reduced to hiring trainees in the hope that one of them would save her bacon. The only positive thing about it was that she didn't have to pay the extortionate wages she previously would have done if they were seasoned professionals.

Before finding out the truth about Bev, Vogue

thought they would go from strength to strength and become a design house of epic proportions, something they had both dreamt of. Having met Bev at university, the two had made an instant connection, seamlessly entering business together. Bev on design, Vogue as the personality for their brand. A great team until the truth came to light.

She's gone now. Let her go.

Within minutes, people slowly filtered into the room and took their seats.

Vogue remained standing at the head of the table, taking a few moments to compose herself. She didn't want to reveal the nervousness that was bubbling below the surface. In the face of adversity, she had to show them they had nothing to fear. That there was a way out. Even if she wasn't a hundred percent sure herself.

All eyes were on Vogue as she began to speak.

'Now, you all know me, and you know I don't beat around the bush when it comes to this business. So it's for this reason only that I'm going to lay all my cards on the table.' Vogue leant forward and put her hands flat on the glass surface. 'Basically, we're fucked.'

The expressions on her employees' faces told her they hadn't expected her to be so truthful.

'Fucked, as in the business is going under and we're going to lose our jobs?' Glenda asked.

'Let's put it this way, if these trainees don't design a new outwear collection that knocks buyers off their feet, then yes, I'm afraid we are.' Vogue paused dramatically as she straightened. 'And when I say we… I mean all of us.'

'Crap! And I've just bought a new flat,' Jake said, sinking back into his seat.

For a moment, Vogue thought he was going to start crying but thankfully he made a quick recovery. The last thing she needed was tears from a grown man. Especially at a time like this.

'And I'm getting married in three months,' John joined in with his woes. 'Judith is going to have kittens when I tell her we might have to scale things down a little.'

Everyone looked at John in disbelief. Scaling things down would still be an extravagant event by anyone else's standards, even Vogue's, and that was saying something.

'Well, thank your lucky stars you haven't just had a baby,' Carol said, patting her stomach.

Vogue held her hands up in the air. 'Whoa, hold on a minute guys. I'm not sharing this with you to make you panic. I'm telling you this so you can prepare yourselves, whatever the outcome. I wouldn't be much of a boss if I didn't let you know what was going on behind the scenes, would I?'

Glenda, the oldest member of her team, shook her head. 'It's a bit ironic that we find out we could be going under on the same day Bev's back in town.'

There was a stunned silence. Vogue's hand automatically rose to the base of her neck and remained there, the pulse pounding against her fingers.

'Oh no, sorry, I thought you knew,' Glenda said, looking around at all the astonished faces staring back at her. 'Jude from accounts is friends with her sister, and you know how she likes to gossip.'

Vogue had to remind herself to take a breath. Her heart pounded against her ribcage with such ferocity, she thought for a moment it might break through.

Although she knew the day would finally come when Bev would show her face again, it seemed like no time at all since the carnage she had left in her wake.

Just then the door opened, and Melissa breezed in, kicking the door shut behind her with her foot. 'What's up? You all look like you've just seen a ghost.'

No one replied, leaving it up to Vogue to share the sudden news.

'She's back!'

Chapter Five

The remaining drive to London was uneventful, not that Amelia would have wanted another car accident, whether it involved a gorgeous woman or not. As she made her way through the chock-a-block city, with its roads packed with cars bumper to bumper, she couldn't help but reflect how different London was to Bournemouth. Not only was the quality of the air vastly inferior but everything seemed to be so… manic. People walked out in front of cars without looking, cyclists appeared from nowhere and motorists seemed more in a hurry than anyone else. Everyone had somewhere important to be. *Probably in a rush to go and pick up a trendy latte from the latest organic coffee shop.* Amelia still couldn't understand the coffee craze that had taken over the UK. She had always been a tea lover and that wasn't going to change anytime soon.

Amelia let out a sigh of relief as she pulled up outside Cecile's house, an hour later than her Sat Nav had predicted. Her T-shirt clung to her clammy back as she climbed out of her car and retrieved her case from the boot. After taking a mouthful of warm water from her water bottle, she made her way up the stairs towards the place she might be calling home for a while. *That's if I get the job.* As much as everyone who saw her work loved it and said what an amazing talent she had, Amelia always felt a little… how could she describe it? Like a fraud. *Imposter syndrome.* That for some reason people were full of compliments to her face but once her back was turned, they were disingenuous about her so-called talent as a fashion designer. Not that this story she made up in her mind had any basis in reality, but her belief was so strong, it was more real to her than reality itself. It was a wonder how she even managed to finish university, considering the level of self-doubt that consumed her.

The door opened and Cecile pulled her into a bear hug as if they'd been estranged for years. To an onlooker, they'd never believe that they'd only parted company a few booze-fuelled hours ago. Not that it showed on Cecile's face. Her flawless skin made her look like she'd just come back from a spa weekend. Tall and blonde, whereas Amelia was average height and brunette, there was a marked contrast between them.

'You made it then,' Cecile said as she guided Amelia inside.

'Just about.'

'Hmmm?' Her attention was no longer focused on Amelia but on her phone.

'I had a bit of an accident,' Amelia said in an attempt to get some kind of reaction from her.

'Hmmm,' Cecile didn't even take the time to look up.

'Yeah, the car's a total right off,' Amelia said in all seriousness as Cecile's eyes seemed to glaze over as if she were in a trance. If Cecile wasn't so attached to her phone, Amelia would happily grab it off her and throw it down the toilet.

'Yeah, there were screeching police cars and...' Amelia threw her hands in the air in frustration. 'I give up.'

'What? Just got like a zillion likes on my Instagram post.' Cecile looked up suddenly coming out of her daydream. 'Sorry, what were you saying?'

'Nothing that's as important as your adoring followers.' As far as Amelia was concerned, mobile phones and social media were the reason for the disconnect between people these days. No one spoke face-to-face anymore and if they did, she always felt there was a sense of urgency to cut the conversation short so they could look at their sodding phone. She dreaded to think what the future held for humanity.

'Sorry, I know I was being rude.'

'It's okay,' Amelia said, suddenly feeling guilty for being judgmental. Would she be so hard on someone fighting an addiction? No, she wouldn't and that's exactly what Cecile and millions of people were suffering from. An invisible addiction to their phones, the difference being they didn't know it.

'Let me knock up some lunch. You must be hungry.'

'I am a bit,' Amelia admitted. The last thing she had eaten was a sandwich but that was hours ago, which was very unlike her. Normally, she had stacks of goodies to accompany her on long drives but after the incident on the motorway, her appetite had seemed to diminish. Thankfully, it was back again with a vengeance.

'Go and unpack. Freshen up.'

'Oooh you sound just like my mum,' Amelia said in jest, but there was some truth in her comment. Even now, her mum always made sure she washed her hands before sitting at the table to eat. It wasn't that her mum was OCD or anything, it was a habit her own mother had drilled into her.

'Do you actually want something to eat?' Cecile raised her eyebrows.

Amelia laughed as she walked away. 'Next you'll be telling me I can't date at work.'

'Trust me. That is one conversation we *will* be having if you get that job,' Cecile said in a tone that let Amelia know that she meant business.

Cecile had never been one to preach or belittle her, or try to bully her under the guise of older meant wiser, even if there was only a couple of years difference between them. In turn, Amelia always took on-board Cecile's advice. So to now hear a warning sign in Cecile's voice gave Amelia some concern.

Instead of continuing, Cecile slipped out of the room and seconds later, Amelia heard activity in the kitchen. It didn't take a genius to figure out now was not the right time for the 'talk' Cecile had in mind. But if it was going to be something along the lines of 'all the employees at Styles are hopping in and out of bed with each other, so steer clear', Amelia would rather not know. Not that she would be even the slightest bit envious that everybody but her seemed to be having sex, it was just that what people did in their private lives had nothing to do with her. And good luck to them if they were getting what she could only fantasise about.

Picking up her case, Amelia carried it to her temporary bedroom. How temporary remained to be seen. She might be back in her car come Wednesday, making the three-hour drive back to Bournemouth.

It didn't take her long to unpack. She had only brought clothes to see her through a couple of days. A tailored grey trouser suit for her interview and a couple of pairs of jeans and tops for daywear. Her intention was to make an overnight trip home to collect the rest of her clothes if she landed the job.

Fifteen minutes later, Amelia was back in the kitchen sat opposite Cecile, eating crab salad and sourdough bread.

'Go on then, out with it,' Amelia said, pouring olive oil over romaine lettuce before taking a mouthful. 'What did you mean with that remark you made earlier? You're not normally this protective.'

'I'm your best friend.' Cecile paused to finish the food in her mouth. 'Besides, in the past I haven't needed to be.'

'Now this sounds intriguing and scary at the same time,' Amelia said wondering what all the drama was about. It was probably one of those things where it was totally blown out of proportion and the actual issue wasn't that important at all.

'Look,' Cecil put her fork down and turned to face Amelia, 'the owner of Styles is gay.'

Amelia jerked back in her seat in mock horror. 'Oh my God! Really?'

Unless Cecile was going to follow up with the revelation that the owner ate lesbians or kept them tied up in her cellar where she tortured them on a daily basis, she couldn't see the relevance of the comment.

'I'm not playing around, I'm being serious.'

'What d'you think she's gonna do? Devour me whole.' Amelia laughed. 'She probably won't even notice I'm alive.'

'That's where you're wrong. Once she sees your designs, sees you, I can guarantee she'll be interested and that scares me.'

Amelia laughed at the thought of any woman being interested in her, let alone a high-powered boss. The idea was so surreal, she would have said her thoughts out loud if it wasn't for the fact that Cecile looked so serious.

'I can assure you, you've got nothing to worry about in that department.'

Cecile picked up her fork and resumed eating. 'Don't say I didn't warn you. You'll lose your head if she gets her claws into you, not to mention your heart.'

Amelia stared at her as a realisation came to the forefront of her mind. Had Cecile witnessed her boss doing something so disturbing that she had to warn Amelia?

'Cecile?' Amelia pressed.

Cecile kept her eyes focused on her food.

Amelia tried again. 'Cecile?'

When she didn't look up, Amelia knew her suspicions were right. But what could be so bad?

Note to self: Keep clear of big bad boss!

Chapter Six

Melissa didn't need to be told who Vogue was referring to. There was only one person that could get under her skin that way – Bev Dawson. She dreaded to think what Vogue had found out.

'I assume it's Bev you're talking about?' Relief flooded Melissa as she plonked herself down on the only empty chair at the table and said a silent prayer of thanks. Everything was okay. There was no need to panic. Besides, Bev wasn't stupid. She would know better than to try and contact Vogue.

Now that the initial fear had passed, Melissa resumed her train of thought. As much as she wanted to, she couldn't get the woman she had met earlier out of her head. It was as if she'd taken a hit of an addictive drug.

Vogue fixed her with a hard stare. 'Yes. Is that all you've got to say?'

'What else is there? We all knew she'd come back one day. It's not like she murdered anyone.'

As soon as the unfiltered words slipped out of her mouth, the room seemed to drop in temperature. But it was too late to backpedal, and in all honesty, Melissa was sick and tired of treading on eggshells around the subject. Yes, Bev's actions had caused a ruckus in the company, but it really was time to move on. It was done. Nothing anyone said or did could change anything and Melissa was sick of pretending she cared.

'Not like she murdered anyone?' Vogue's words were cold and precise. 'And you think that makes it okay?'

'I didn't say that, but I think we've got more important things to worry about, don't you?' Melissa mentally braced herself for the onslaught that never came.

Instead, Vogue turned her attention back to the rest of the group. 'Melissa's right, we can't afford to be off our game. Not now. We need to focus.'

'So what's the plan?' John said.

'I'm interviewing potential trainees. We'll hire three of the best. If they can't help dig us out of this hole, no one will.'

'When're the interviews?' Lindsay asked, looking relieved Vogue had a plan of action.

'Tomorrow,' Vogue said with full gusto.

Like that's going to make any difference.

Melissa stifled a yawn. It amused her to think Vogue thought she was going to be able to scrape through and come out on top. Yes, Melissa had seen her do it many times before, but things were different now. The industry had changed rapidly. There was now a relentless conveyor belt of fashion designs at bargain basement prices. The idea of tapping into a new market with jackets and coats was laughable, but who was she to shatter Vogue's pie in the sky fantasy?

'What space will the newbies be using?' Jake asked, trying to hide his agitation. It made Melissa wonder how he managed to make it into work each day, let alone spend his time interacting with people. Jake was a self-confessed 'human hater' and he made no bones about his disdain for all those that weren't covered in fur.

'The offices on the second floor,' Vogue said.

'Oh, so that's why there's been so much activity going on down there?' Carol chipped in.

Melissa watched on as Vogue took questions from the team, answering each of them flawlessly with the confidence of a true leader. Only Melissa could tell she was apprehensive about the future. Vogue hated failure. Hated not getting what she wanted. And that's why the company had been such a success, because Vogue was as ruthless as they came.

Not that it was such a bad thing. Had circumstances been different, Melissa might have actually liked Vogue. Admired her even. Bonded with her over the many things they had in common. But there was no way of turning back the clock. *It is what it is.*

Nevertheless, the façade would all be over soon, so thinking about what could have been was totally irrelevant. The next phase in Melissa's life would be stress-free. Where she would be able to go on holiday and not have to worry every time her phone rang. Not have to fear it was Vogue with another drama that involved needing Melissa to drop everything and hop on the next plane home. That she could wake up in the morning and not be mired in bitterness and resentment.

No, once Vogue got what she had coming to her, Melissa was going to walk away and never look back.

'So if no one has any more questions, I suggest we

all get back to doing what we do best. Work,' Vogue said.

There was a low mumble of conversation as chairs were pushed back, and her colleagues filed out of the room.

'Do you think I've lost their confidence?' Vogue asked, tactfully avoiding any eye contact.

Melissa had never heard Vogue sound so unsure of herself before. She got up and walked to Vogue's side.

'They know this isn't your fault. If you weren't still at the helm, this place would've gone down like a sinking ship. They trust you. I trust you.'

Vogue studied Melissa intently for a moment, then opened her mouth to say something before promptly shutting it. Melissa wondered if Vogue could detect the insincerity of her words. That it almost choked her to say them. Every time she buoyed Vogue up with false flattery, it literally made her hate herself.

That was why she had escalated things.

Melissa really didn't know how much more she could take.

Chapter Seven

Blood pounded in Vogue's ears. She hated to think what her blood pressure reading would have been if a doctor had taken it at that exact moment in time. Probably in the danger zone. Drinking champagne at one o'clock in the afternoon certainly wasn't helping matters. Instead of soothing her nerves, the alcohol gave her internal rage extra fuel.

'Most of these are fucking useless! Fifteen so-called designers and this is all they can come up with?' Vogue swiped the pile of papers on the desk onto the floor, finally allowing the growing frustration to get to her. 'You might as well give them all a box of crayons and a colouring pad.'

Melissa leant over in her seat, gathered the papers into a pile and put them on the desk. 'They aren't that bad. Some were pretty good.'

'You think?' Vogue grabbed the papers and thrust them back into Melissa's hand. 'Take another look. Would you buy this shit? Put our brand on any of them?'

Under normal circumstances, Vogue would never have been so dismissive of someone's work. No matter how mediocre it was in her eyes. The fact was, none of the designs were 'bad' just because she didn't like them, but given her current situation, she couldn't afford to be blasé about the distinctive stamp she needed to make an impact.

What she thought would be a quick prep for the

interviews the following day had turned into more despair. Why hadn't she sifted the applications herself? *Because I had no time!*

Melissa leafed through the sheets of paper, studying each of them closely. Reaching the last design, Melissa shook her head dismally.

'These two I would but the rest probably not. They were the best out of all the applications we had.'

'So if we don't like them, why the hell would women who are looking for a brand they can identify with? Jesus!' Vogue sat on the edge of her desk. 'I might as well call it a day now. Save myself the humiliation of being forced into bankruptcy.'

It was bad enough trying to hide the fact that she was struggling to make ends meet. Vogue didn't know how much longer she could carry on the façade of being financially abundant. She was grateful that she still had close friends outside the industry who knew the truth and were willing to help her out. Such as her friend Greg, who had graciously provided the champagne and lobsters for the gifts she was sending out to her top clients. It was something she did every year for a select few. If she failed to do so this year, they would immediately know something was amiss.

It had never occurred to Vogue to come clean about her situation in the hope of gaining their support. The fashion industry was a jungle and if her competitors smelt blood, they would go in for the kill without a second thought.

'Maybe closing the doors is something you should

seriously be thinking about. There's no point hiring people just for the sake of it. It will only cause you more stress. Also, getting everyone's hopes up that they'll still have a job in a few months isn't fair. Maybe it's time to face the fact that a knight in shining armour isn't going to come in and save the day.'

'I know what you're saying makes sense, but I can't give up when there's still that small part of me that thinks I can do it. I have to, otherwise what's it all been about?' Vogue said, running her fingers through her hair. 'Every day of my life I've struggled. Every fucking day. And when I finally think I've made it, that I can ease my foot off the pedal for once, I'm hit by a sodding train.'

'D'you think you're being a tad over dramatic? You won't be the first person to fail, Vogue, and you sure as hell won't be the last. And I'm saying this objectively – if you carry on the way you're going, you'll literally have nothing. So quitting while you've still got a roof over your head might be the best thing to do.'

Vogue raised her eyebrows. Despite Melissa being the best personal assistant she'd ever had, they were poles apart when it came to the fear factor. Melissa was all about playing it safe. To only jump when there was a safety net to fall into. Whereas, Vogue's way was to act first and think about the consequences later.

Bev had been exactly the same which is why they worked so well together. *Don't even go there. Everything I thought about her was a lie! Probably our friendship as well.* Pushing the intrusive thoughts out of her mind, Vogue turned her attention to the matter at hand.

'I'll never quit,' Vogue said, the anger and frustration slowly subsiding as her inner strength rose. 'The thing is, I should never have relied on just one designer. All of this is of my own doing. My mum once told me to never rely on what only one person brought to the table. God, I wish I would've taken her advice.'

'Yes, you should've. Your mum sounds like a wise woman,' Melissa said, smiling.

'She was. If it wasn't for her, I don't know where I would've ended up. She gave me so much encouragement to follow my dreams. I suppose that's why I can't let go now. She wouldn't have wanted me to. She would've told me, if I had to go down, I should go down fighting.'

'I'm sure she didn't mean to the point of self-destruction because that's where you're heading. You've seen the accounts, so you know how bad things are.'

'Yeah, so you keep saying.' Vogue broke off when there was a knock at the door. 'Come in.'

Damien from HR walked in carrying a folder in his hand. His broad shoulders and bulky build made him look like he should be on a rugby pitch, not working in an office pushing papers all day.

'Hey, Vogue, how's it going?'

'Good. Yourself?'

'Can't complain.' Damien handed the folder to Vogue. 'This woman's name is on the interview list for the trainees, her names Amelia. I just found her designs in my drawer, they somehow got mixed up with my other paperwork.'

'Oh okay, thanks.'

Damien gave Melissa a nod of acknowledgment before he quickly left.

Vogue wasn't going to set her expectations too high after what she had seen already, but she could live in hope. As she slowly turned each page, that familiar sense of excitement rose in her. Exactly the same way it used to when Bev would turn up at her house at three in the morning, bursting with enthusiasm about a design she had just come up with. Despite the early hour of the morning, they would drink copious amounts of coffee and dissect every aspect of the design, from the colours to the cut, right down to the material and buttons. They were fun and exciting times.

That was part of the relationship she still missed with Bev.

'Look at these,' Vogue said once she reached the last design. She didn't want to sound too excited until she heard Melissa's thoughts. For some reason, she was doubting her own judgement. Probably because she was desperate for a light at the end of the very dark, dank tunnel she found herself in, and couldn't believe she might have found it.'

Melissa took the folder and flicked through the designs, her eyes slowly digesting them. 'Okay, I'll admit this one has got a little potential—'

'A little—'

'What do you want me to say? That she's amazing. I'm sorry but I just don't see it myself,' Melissa said.

Vogue raised the glass to her mouth then thought

better of it, placing it back down. *This is not the way to go.* She had seen so many others turn to alcohol in order to ease the pressure, and she really didn't want to become one of them.

If Melissa couldn't see the potential, that didn't mean it wasn't there. Like Vogue always said, taste was subjective. Never more so than when it came to fashion.

'Oh really, Ms. Fashion police?'

'Yes, really. I mean this one isn't that bad, but it's nothing special.' Melissa held the design up for Vogue to see.

Vogue tilted her head as she took in the design Melissa was holding. It was one that she thought was particularly good. So good that it fit perfectly with her image of the outwear collection. There was something very down to earth about Amelia's style. As if her intention wasn't to be showy, instead to be practical with a trendy touch. The colours weren't too brash, yet they weren't dull. She seemed to have a knack at getting the absolute balance right. There was something eye-catching about the design of the clothes, so much so, Vogue could actually envisage her target audience wearing them.

Vogue took the folder back and laid it on her desk. The dark cloud that had been covering her world recently, suddenly began to lift. Distancing itself further and further away from her until she almost felt giddy with excitement.

'This woman has talent,' Vogue said, mostly to herself, as she tapped the folder with the tip of her finger. 'Get her in for an interview today.'

Melissa's eyes widened. 'I... I thought the interviews were tomorrow.'

'I want to see her today. And I want you to keep this under your hat, I don't want anyone else knowing she's coming in.'

'Okay, you're the boss.' Melissa rose to her feet and walked wearily out of the room.

Vogue watched her go and felt a sense of regret about the situation they all found themselves in. Melissa in particular. She really didn't blame her for feeling disheartened about the way things had turned out. After all, she had been the driving force in advising Vogue against paying out damages to the student whose work Bev had stolen. As much as she tried to make Melissa see things from her point of view, Melissa had been adamant that if the truth got out about the pay-out, it could start an avalanche of fresh allegations, especially if it wasn't the first time Bev had copied someone else's work.

It was a moot point as far as Vogue was concerned. She knew it was the only time Bev had done something that stupid. How did she know? Even at the time, when Bev showed her the designs, Vogue knew, no, not knew – felt something was amiss. First, alarm bells sounded due to Bev's lack of enthusiasm for the work. Looking back, Vogue remembered how detached she was from it. And Bev was never detached from her creations. Never.

Alarm bell number two should have been the loudest, and Vogue still couldn't fathom out why she ignored it. Even today, she remembered the ferocity with which her gut tried to warn her that something was amiss with Bev's designs. The style, the textures, the whole concept just felt off. Unlike the designs that were hidden away in the folder next to her.

Unable to help herself, Vogue picked up the folder again and brought out the sheets of paper. Using her index finger, she followed the outline of the sketch, feeling it as if it were real.

'Now this is what I'm talking about,' Vogue said aloud as she looked heavenward. 'Thank you, God!'

If this woman could reproduce several designs of the same calibre for her outwear collection, Vogue's business may have just been saved.

Chapter Eight

The shock must have been evident on Amelia's face because Cecile was staring at her with an expression of concern. Finishing the call, Amelia slowly put the phone down on the table. She couldn't bear to look at the food she'd been enjoying only minutes earlier. Her stomach was in knots.

Amelia really didn't want to share the details from the call. She knew as soon as she told Cecile, she would be all over it, telling her how right she was. Which really didn't make much sense, as the owner had never laid eyes on Amelia before. The only question burning at the back of her mind, was why would her interview have been moved forward a day? Was that a good sign? Or were they interviewing the weak candidates first in order to filter them out?

'What's wrong?' Cecile asked, her eyes boring into Amelia's, seeking an answer to her question.

'Oh, um nothing.' Amelia's mind raced, trying to find a way to avoid lying whilst not actually telling the truth. She was excited regardless of why they wanted to see her now, and she didn't want Cecile to put a downer on it.

'The expression on your face isn't saying "it's nothing".' Cecile rested her chin on her open palm, giving the impression that if she had to sit there all day to extract the truth from Amelia, she would.

'Oh, all right,' Amelia said. 'But I swear to God, I don't want to hear "I told you so" come out of your mouth.'

Cecile smiled and pretended to zip her mouth shut.

Feeling assured Cecile would respect her wishes, Amelia said, 'That was Vogue's personal assistant.'

True to her nonverbal agreement, Cecile was silent for a few moments before finally saying, 'And? What did she want?'

'For me to go in for my interview today. Now.' Amelia hesitated, unaware of how Cecile was going to take the next part. 'Vogue wants to meet me.'

'I knew it!' Cecile pushed back her chair and jumped to her feet. 'I told you, didn't I?'

'Calm down. You promised you wouldn't do this.'

'I know but Jesus, that woman is so fucking predictable.'

'Don't you think you're slightly overreacting. She hasn't invited me back to her house. She wants to meet me at her office to discuss my designs.'

'Yeah of course she does, that's how it all starts.'

'I've never met her, how would she even know I'm gay?' Amelia asked. 'And I'm not being funny but if she's as bad as you say she is, why are you still working for her?'

Cecile frowned. When she spoke, it looked as if it was a struggle to force the words out of her mouth. 'Firstly, she's probably looked you up on social media and secondly, I have bills to pay.'

'Then look for another job,' Amelia fired back at her straight away.

'I can't—'

'Can't or won't?'

'It's not that easy,' Cecile said quietly after a pause.

Still unable to justify why she would remain working for a woman she clearly detested, Cecile's answer didn't hold any weight with Amelia. If she had a valid reason, Amelia would understand, but to tell her absolutely nothing and just expect her to blindly trust her judgement, she couldn't do that. Not even for Cecile.

'Well unless you can tell me what she's done and how it affected you personally, I think I'll reserve my judgement of her until we meet.'

Cecile looked as if Amelia had struck her, but it wasn't Amelia's intention to hurt her with the comment. It was simply that this was her professional life and she wanted to remain as detached from work dramas as possible. She had seen first-hand what happened to her colleagues that became too familiar with their bosses, only to find themselves shut out when it all turned sour.

'Okay, well I'm coming with you.'

Amelia gasped. The thought of taking a friend to an interview with her was unthinkable. What if they were seen together? It would make her look like a child who needed looking after, not a grown woman who was quite capable of standing on her own two feet.

'There's no way on this earth you're coming with me.'

'Listen—'

'No, Cecile, listen to yourself. You're not being rational,' Amelia said, trying to reason with her. 'How d'you think it would look if I turned up to a meeting with my best friend? I'd look incompetent. Not to mention if it's with someone who works there.'

'Suppose you're right.' Cecile sighed, apparently coming to her senses. 'Just promise me you won't accept her offer if she asks you out for a drink.'

Now she really has lost the plot! Amelia tried to imagine in what parallel universe something like that would ever happen. Where you went for a job interview and at the end the interviewer randomly asked you out for a drink. It was so outlandish, she couldn't believe someone as level-headed as Cecile would even think like that.

'I think you're getting ahead of yourself now. I really don't think a potential employer is going to hit on me at an interview.'

Cecile gave her a satisfied smirk. 'You don't know Vogue.'

Though Amelia was grateful Cecile was looking out for her, she found her reaction to the whole situation a tad strange. It wasn't as if she was a wet behind the ears eighteen-year-old who had just left home. She was a mature woman who was quite capable of looking after herself. Warding of unwanted attention wasn't going to be a problem for her. She was not afraid to use the word 'no'. Even against her boss. *Boss?* Amelia realised she was being presumptive. She hadn't even met the woman yet, let alone gained employment with her company. Though it couldn't hurt to adopt a positive attitude. After all, what else did she have?

Talent, a small voice reminded her. But even with a talent such as hers, Amelia knew if she didn't get any exposure, it would go to waste, and she'd be doing menial work for the rest of her life.

'No, I don't and by the sounds of it she's not someone I'd like to know on a personal level, but this is business. I'm not going there to make friends.'

'Suit yourself,' Cecile said with a sour note to her voice.

'Come on, Cecile, be happy for me.' Amelia walked over to her and took her hands in her own. 'If it wasn't for you, I wouldn't have even got an interview. Don't spoil things for me.'

Cecile's eyes narrowed. 'I'm not trying to. I just don't want to see you get hurt.'

'I won't. Look, how about this. Why don't we actually wait and see if I get picked, and then we can talk strategy about keeping the boss at a distance. Deal?'

'Right, now that's sorted, I'd better go and get ready. Don't want to start off on the wrong foot.'

Amelia waited until she was in her room before she finally felt the tension in her shoulders relax. Although she knew Cecile's intention wasn't to put the fear of God into her, she was feeling slightly apprehensive. For all her bravado, did Amelia really want to work for a woman whose behaviour bordered on what could be seen as sexual harassment?

More importantly, if she was offered the position,

would she have the guts to turn down such a life changing opportunity? Amelia had done so in the past when her previous boss had 'accidentally' put his hand on her knee, only for her to push it off and for him to replace it. Okay, the job in question had been in retail and she couldn't have cared less if she'd been fired, but Styles? That was playing with the big guns. This was all about her getting the job on merit for original creativity.

In the end, Amelia told herself to get a grip and see how things played out. For all she knew, she might be heading back to Bournemouth with her tail between her legs within the next few days, and then what would she do? Continue slaving away at a day job she hated, while trying to find the energy at night to design a collection that no one was ever going to see?

Amelia walked over to the wardrobe and took out her suit. It was one of her most recent designs. She'd even sewed it. Admittedly, it had taken her weeks to get the hang of using the sewing machine, but with determination and persistence, she had mastered it and was proud of herself for doing so.

That was what mattered to her at the end of the day, doing something she loved. That she found great pleasure in. So no, she wasn't going to be put off by the thought of a lechy boss, no matter who she was.

Applying make-up in the mirror, Amelia took a step back and admired the way it made her seem like another person altogether. That's why she liked to wear so much, to hide the real her. That way if she was rejected, she wouldn't take it personally. After all, it was her fake persona that she was showing to the world. Not the unsure little girl that resided in an adult's body.

Amelia pasted a smile onto her face and pulled her shoulders back to give herself more height and the look of someone who meant business. She then planted her hands on her hips in a Wonder Woman pose. *If it works for Wonder Woman, it can work for me.*

Although the smile looked convincing and her body gave an air of confidence, on closer inspection, the smile didn't reach her eyes and the tension showed between her eyebrows.

Amelia smoothed out the frown line with her finger. She couldn't lose courage now. She had to quieten those voices of self-doubt if she was going to get this job.

Still staring at herself in the mirror, Amelia watched as tears brimmed beneath her eye lashes until they began to drop, leaving a trail in the thick layer of her foundation.

This was all wrong. All of it.

Sniffing as she tugged a face wipe out of its packaging, Amelia rubbed at her face until every last trace of her make-up was gone and all that remained was her slightly reddened skin.

She was done! Done with hiding. Done with fearing rejection. Done with not ever feeling good enough. And most importantly, done with trying to be someone she wasn't.

Why couldn't she just be happy and accept that she was going to be rejected by people? Wasn't it better to be true to herself regardless? To love herself unconditionally, in a way that no other human could?

If the world at large was going to accept her, they would have to accept the real her, warts and all.

Throwing cold water over her face to sooth her now red skin, Amelia patted her face with a towel. Looking at herself directly in the mirror, she smiled. This time a genuine one straight from her heart.

Wonder Woman wouldn't sell herself short.

And neither would Amelia.

Chapter Nine

Melissa waited in the air-conditioned lobby of the building. Despite the cool temperature, a bead of sweat rolled down her back, leaving a ticklish sensation that she was eager to scratch but couldn't quite reach.

Better to concentrate on that then think about Vogue pacing the floor upstairs in her office, waiting for a miracle to happen. She checked her watch again for the fifth time in as many minutes. Anxious wasn't the word. When she'd spoken to Amelia, the designer whose work Vogue had actually liked, she'd tried her best to sound as disinterested as possible. To give off a bad enough vibe that would have the woman debating whether she wanted to work in a company where the staff sounded miserable and dissatisfied. To her dismay, the woman wasn't put off in the slightest which had pissed her off to no end.

Knowing that she had no choice, Melissa had told Amelia to jump in a cab and make her way over ASAP. The sooner it was over with, the better.

Melissa still couldn't figure out how Amelia's work had got into the mix. Vogue had given her the job of sifting through the applications and arranging the interviews. She had removed all of the decent applicants, so it should have been simple enough to talk Vogue out of going any further with her plan to revamp the company with new designers if they were all useless. How had the best application been held up in HR? And how on earth did she get on the interview list when Melissa hadn't even seen her designs?

Melissa had managed to stop herself from laughing at Vogue's expression when she saw the other crap people had sent in? But that smile had soon been wiped off her face when Damien walked in with the work of a designer who, under normal circumstances, Melissa would have been in awe of.

She had to give Vogue some credit. She had an eye for talent. Even with Melissa trying to talk Amelia down, Vogue had stuck to her guns, the stubborn fool that she was.

Melissa stood and straightened her clothes, convinced that the taxi that had just pulled up outside the building would be carrying the woman she was waiting for.

Within a few minutes, a woman walked through the door and Melissa did a double take as the woman she assumed was Amelia, looked around her impressive surroundings in awe. Melissa's eyes narrowed. She'd met Amelia before.

But where? Brunette, very attractive...

As Amelia neared, Melissa could see recognition in her eyes which Melissa couldn't help but notice were framed with dark long lashes.

'I didn't think we'd meet again so soon.' Amelia outstretched her hand and Melissa took it, slowly shaking it.

Jesus, it's Ms Daydreamer, Melissa realised with a

shock as their earlier encounter started to filter into her brain. Melissa drew her hand back a little too quickly, eager not to let Amelia feel her tremble. If Amelia had noticed Melissa's reaction to her touch, her eyes didn't portray the slightest hint of any emotion. In fact, her expressionless gaze remained on Melissa.

And what eyes. A soft sigh escaped Melissa's lips.

'Do you remember me?' Amelia suddenly said, breaking the spell.

'What? Yes of course,' Melissa replied. 'You crashed into me this morning.'

Please tell me this isn't happening! It can't be. What was the likelihood of the woman she couldn't get out of her mind, being on the interview list for a job at her place of work?

'I think crashed is a bit harsh,' Amelia said, cutting straight into her thoughts.

'Okay, more like bumped.'

Amelia's eyes danced with amusement. 'So you work here?'

'Yes, I'm the one that called you.'

'I thought your voice sounded familiar, but I'd never have guessed it was you.'

How could Melissa not have recognised her voice? *I suppose people sound different on the phone.* But then again why would she think for one second that it would be Amelia? Melissa would have thought there was more chance of her winning the lottery than bumping into Amelia again in a city with over eight million people in it.

'You sound disappointed?' Melissa said.

Amelia's cheeks flushed which Melissa saw as a good sign. Either she was embarrassed or… did she let herself dare to dream and put it down to nervousness because she felt something towards Melissa too?

'Not disappointed,' Amelia said, giving Melissa a smile that sent her pulse racing. 'More like surprised. In a nice way.'

'I'm glad to hear it.'

Melissa was so busy trying to think of what to say next, she totally forgot the reason for calling Amelia in the first place. It was only when her phone started ringing that she came back down to earth with a crash.

'That'll be Vogue,' Melissa said, referring to her phone as she pressed the ignore button. 'Suppose we'd better go up.'

'Lead the way.'

Melissa didn't miss the way Amelia's gaze ran over her face and down to her chest then back. *It seems the attraction really is mutual. Finally, things are starting to look up.*

As they rode up in the lift, Melissa half-heartedly engaged in small talk with one of the managers she frequently liaised with. In her peripheral view, she could just make out Amelia eyeing her slowly and thoroughly.

She was grateful when the lift stopped, and the doors opened. The intensity caused by the close proximity proving too much for her.

'So how long have you worked here?' Amelia asked.

Melissa turned to look at her briefly to see if she was genuinely interested or was just making small talk for the sake of it. By the look on her face it seemed she was interested.

'Oh, around a year,' Melissa said, partly because she couldn't actually remember how long she'd been under Vogue's thumb, and partly because she didn't want to remember.

'And you still enjoy it?'

Now how do I answer that? The truth or a big whopping lie?

In the end, she decided against telling her the truth. If Amelia was given the job, she didn't know who she would become pally with. God forbid it was Vogue. If Vogue ever found out how Melissa really felt towards her, she thought Vogue would probably die from shock. It pleased Melissa to know all those years at drama school hadn't gone to waste.

'Let's just say I enjoy parts of it,' Melissa said and left it at that.

Before Amelia could enquire any further, Melissa pushed the door open to Vogue's office and stood aside to let Amelia enter first.

On hearing the door open, Vogue who was standing with her back to the room, turned. Melissa swallowed an internal sigh when she caught sight of Vogue's eyebrows rise in interest at seeing Amelia.

Fucking great! I don't even get a look in for five minutes.

As much as Melissa would have liked to excuse herself from the room, she couldn't. She needed to see what played out between Vogue and Amelia. If she was going to pursue Amelia, she needed to know what she was up against. Vogue wasn't going to win this one without a fight.

In the past, Melissa had let go of the things she wanted too easily. Whether it be women, arguments, decision making – the list went on. She had been subservient for one reason and one reason only. Melissa didn't want to upset the applecart. It served her purpose to remain under the radar. That way there was never a chance for her to be fired or pushed out of Vogue's inner circle.

She needed to remain in her position so she could right the wrong that had been served up to her for no reason other than pig-headedness, and probably jealousy.

Melissa looked from Vogue to Amelia and her heart sank even further. It was obvious the attraction was mutual by the way Amelia's fair cheeks blushed, and her fingers immediately twirled her hair.

What was it about Vogue that made her attract most women she came into contact with? Yes, she was beautiful, there was no denying that, but what was it about her personality that drew them in? She found Vogue too bullish for her liking. Too domineering. The need to be in control was almost suffocating. It was no wonder that the longer she worked for Vogue, the higher her intake of alcohol was. It was the only way she could survive. She needed something to block out the constant chatter in her mind and she didn't want to turn to drugs. Illegal or legal.

Melissa crossed her arms over her chest and

watched the exchange between the two women play out in front of her. The atmosphere in the room, which half an hour ago was lacklustre, now buzzed with an intense excitement.

The prey and its kill.

Melissa motioned Amelia forward to take a seat and she followed suit.

Vogue slowly made her way back to her desk, her eyes gleaming with curiosity as they remained still transfixed on Amelia, as if she would simply vanish into thin air if she let her out of her sight.

'Amelia,' Vogue said, lowering herself into her seat.

'The one and only,' Amelia said then quickly covered her mouth with her hand as if realising that she had forgotten her place.

Melissa smiled to herself. She liked Amelia's energy. Her innocence and playfulness were a refreshing combination.

'I hope there's only one of you,' Vogue said, smiling.

Melissa inwardly groaned as Amelia giggled.

Jesus Christ, the mind boggles.

The staring between the women continued, prompting Melissa to clear her throat loudly. 'I think we should get straight to the point, don't you, Vogue?'

Vogue barely glanced at her. 'I suppose we better had.'

'Amelia, as you must know, we're looking for three trainees to help design our new outwear collection—'

'Sounds very exciting,' Amelia said, cutting Vogue

short before she'd finished her sentence.

Vogue smiled at her, obviously taking her interruption as a sign that she was eager about working for her.

'It is, for the potential trainee as well as ourselves, obviously,' Vogue said keeping her eyes trained on Amelia as if she'd disappear if she didn't.

Vogue glanced at Melissa briefly before turning her full attention back to Amelia.

Uh oh, here we go. She's going in for the kill.

The poor woman didn't stand a chance. She'd been in the room less than five minutes and Vogue looked like she was going to make a play for her. This, despite not know whether the woman was straight or not. Melissa didn't think she was but that was beside the point. It was unprofessional to behave in that manner. Melissa may have been guilty of attempting to flirt with Amelia, but she wasn't her potential boss.

'So, tell me Amelia, why do you think you fit the bill?'

Amelia straightened in her seat and was just about to answer when Vogue interrupted her.

'Actually, why don't you tell me as I show you around?' Vogue pushed herself to her feet.

Amelia smiled sweetly at Vogue then at Melissa. 'I'd love for you both to show me around.'

Melissa bowed her head in order to hide her grin. She had thwarted Vogue's attempt at alone time. The first woman to ever do that since she had known Vogue. Normally, they succumbed to her charm straight away. But not Amelia it seemed.

Something tells me I'm really going to like this woman.

Chapter Ten

The interview had gone better than expected. Amelia was a great candidate for the trainee position and although Vogue was a hundred percent sure she would hire her, she wanted to meet the other applicants before making a rash decision. What had impressed her though was her passion and knowledge for not only the creative side of fashion, but the whole industry.

She had done her homework regarding Styles and it showed when asked how she thought she could fit in with their brand, 'by making it so distinctive that anybody seeing your badge, knows who you are.'

That answer had been good enough for Vogue, but she had to wonder why Melissa didn't seem to be very keen on her. Even though Melissa was her PA, Vogue liked to have her as a sounding board, which meant having a second opinion on things in case she missed something.

Vogue knew Melissa wasn't keen on Amelia's designs, but she couldn't fault her as a genuinely nice and capable woman.

Vogue waited until the lift doors closed and Amelia disappeared from view before she let out a low whistle.

'So, what did you think?'
'She's all right.'
'Just all right?'

'Tell me what you want me to say and I'll say it.' Melissa started walking back in the direction of her office.

Vogue stared after her, unsure if she'd heard right. Was Melissa implying that Vogue wanted 'yes' people around her? For her to agree with everything she said and not have an opinion of their own? If so, when the hell had that got into her mind? Wanting people to agree with her was not how Vogue worked. She liked sharing ideas and hearing other opinions. The fact that the choice lay with her at the end was only because she was the one who had to take the flack if things went wrong. Like they had with Bev.

'Hey, hold up a second,' Vogue called out as she slowly jogged behind her. 'What the hell did you mean by that comment?'

'Nothing. I gave my opinion, but you kept pressing so next time I'll just tell you what you want to hear.'

'If it came across like that, I'm sorry. I just want to try and understand what you didn't like about her.'

Melissa stopped abruptly. 'Look, you fancy her.'

Vogue held up her hands. 'Whoa… where did that come from?'

'Come on, Vogue, don't you think you were being obvious?'

'Obvious? What are you going on about?' Vogue tried to recall if she'd stepped out of line or said anything inappropriate, but nothing came to mind. She wasn't going to deny that she found Amelia attractive. But to suggest she would use her position as an employer to proposition someone was crazy. She had never behaved that way in her life and wasn't about to start now. No matter how pretty the woman was.

They resumed walking again. Vogue remained silent as they entered her office. She went straight over to her desk and switched off her laptop.

'What're you doing?' Melissa asked.

'Going for a drink. I'm done for the day.'

Melissa's accusation had left her agitated. As if she was a predator of some sort.

'But what about Amelia? Are you going to hire her?'

Vogue looked up at Melissa and saw none of the maliciousness in her eyes evident earlier. 'I haven't decided yet. I'll make my decision tomorrow.'

'You're the boss,' Melissa said, smiling. 'D'you want company?'

Vogue raised her eyebrows. She had noticed a pattern with Melissa recently. Where one minute she would behave normally as in friendly, approachable and even on the odd occasion joyous. The next, she showed signs of a darker side to her personality. Vogue had seen her getting short with staff members when Melissa thought no one was looking. On the odd occasion, she had even snapped at Vogue before quickly apologizing. It was if she was holding something in. Vogue had put it down to frustration at the thought of the business failing, but she wasn't too sure about that anymore. It seemed to run a lot deeper.

She slipped into her jacket and brushed past

Melissa. 'See you in the morning.'

Vogue made her way down to the garage and was soon seated in her BMW. Her nerves were on edge. She was going to have a serious talk with Melissa and give her the chance to air any grievances she felt towards her. If Vogue was going to fight to save her company, she needed to have everyone on-board. If they weren't, then she'd have to let them go, which was a shame because she genuinely liked Melissa. Okay, so they weren't close friends – both women being too different for that to happen, but Vogue respected her and the attributes she brought to her job, but that wasn't enough to keep her on if things carried on the way they were.

As Vogue drove the short distance to the bar, she replayed Melissa's comments about Amelia. Vogue had to admit she had taken a liking to her. But not in the way Melissa had misinterpreted. One couldn't help who they were attracted to, and if she decided to hire Amelia, she would treat her the same way she treated everyone at her company. That way there was no chance of professional boundaries being blurred. In that moment, she realised that she would be mad not to hire Amelia, regardless of the attraction.

Making her way into BH1, the usual haunt for the staff at Styles, Vogue took a cursory glance around the dim bar. The place looked like a ghost town.

'Hey, V, usual?' the barwoman said, coming to a standstill in front of her.

'Please.'

'How's it goin'?' The barwoman poured vodka

over ice and slid the drink in front of Vogue.

'Let's just say it's going.' Vogue paid for her drink and slid an extra note across the bar as a tip. 'Thanks, Tara.'

'No, thank you,' Tara said, slipping the note into her pocket. 'No Lindsay tonight?'

'Nope.'

Despite having moved on from her conversation with Melissa, for some reason Amelia remained stuck in Vogue's mind. She wasn't thinking of anything in particular about her, just vague random thoughts, like how much she would have liked to have spent more time in her company. Not for a sexual encounter but to talk. Her enthusiasm about the fashion industry reminded her of Bev, and feeling as vulnerable as she did, she wouldn't have minded a little of the familiar.

Amelia isn't Bev. No, she wasn't but she had made a massive impact on her in the short space of time they'd spent together. Maybe Melissa saw what Vogue was trying to deny.

Vogue took a mouthful of her drink and knocked it back. A few more of them and Amelia would be a distant memory. Just where she deserved to be. The last thing she needed was to develop another crush on her employee.

Four drinks later, despite her best effort, Vogue was still having difficulty getting Amelia out of her mind. Convinced it was because she triggered a need for her to connect with someone who had as much passion for the business as she did, she went a little easier on herself.

Vogue kept her annoyance in check when a woman nudged her shoulder as she pushed herself into the space between Vogue and another woman at the bar, causing her to spill her fifth drink.

'Oh shit, sorry,' the woman said over the music. Vogue had been so caught up in her mental conflict that she hadn't even realised the bar had been filling up.

'Don't worry a—' Vogue stopped mid-sentence as she inadvertently inhaled the aroma of the woman's sweet perfume. It was a familiar scent.

Slowly, she turned to look up at the woman and Vogue's stomach knotted up in discomfort.

Cecile. The last woman she'd had a one-night stand with. The curious straight woman who had tried to entice Vogue into a secretive love affair, all because she didn't want her friends or family to know she'd had sex with a woman.

To say Vogue had been insulted would have been an understatement but she kind of knew where Cecile was coming from. It couldn't be easy to reach your forties and find out that your whole life had been a lie. But as much as she sympathised, Vogue was not up for being anyone's dirty little secret. She had too much pride and self-respect.

'Vogue!' Cecile said, pushing her hair back from her face. Though the move was casual, the glare in her eyes was anything but.

'Cecile.'

'What're you doing here?' Cecile asked, looking around behind her nervously.

Vogue raised her eyebrows at her glass. 'Drinking. Last time I checked that's what bars were for.'

'I—'

'There you are.' Another familiar voice, but this one sent her heart racing. 'You could've waited for me.'

Vogue turned around and looked straight into the eyes of the woman she had tried and failed to get out of her mind all evening.

'Oh, Vogue,' Amelia said. 'Um, nice to see you again.'

Vogue swallowed hard. 'Can I get you a drink?'

'She's fine,' Cecile interrupted before Amelia could respond.

Amelia's cheeks coloured as she looked between Cecile and Vogue respectively. 'Sorry, she didn't—'

'Don't worry. Whatever she meant is no skin off my nose.' Vogue swallowed back the rest of her drink and placed the glass on the bar. She stared at Cecile. 'Now, if you'll excuse me, I have a date with my bed.'

Vogue turned and attempted to squeeze by Amelia without touching her but that proved impossible. For a split second, their bodies became one. The heat between them instantaneous.

Vogue stumbled slightly as she drew away and headed for the entrance. She hadn't planned on drinking so much. She was going to have to leave her car behind and get a taxi which was a pain in the arse. It meant she would have to drop by the bar at six a.m. when the parking restrictions started, but first she needed to get her phone out of her car to call a taxi. Sauntering over to it, Vogue had just opened the door when she felt it swing back out of her hand. Confused, she turned around.

'You're not thinking of driving, are you?' Amelia said from a few feet away.

'What?' Vogue asked, feeling slightly confused.

'Drink driving?'

Vogue laughed. 'No, of course not, I was getting my phone to call a cab.'

'Sorry—'

'You say that a lot, don't you?' Vogue said, holding onto the edge of the car as the alcohol seeped through her system making her unsteady on her feet. Drinking on an empty stomach hadn't been one of her brightest ideas.

Vogue looked up as the clouds opened and a deluge of rain came out of nowhere. Before she knew what was happening, Amelia had her arm around Vogue's waist gently guiding her into the passenger seat, before taking her car keys out of her hand and running around to the driver's side.

'Put your seat belt on,' Amelia ordered.

Not needing to be told twice, Vogue slid the belt across her chest.

'Are you taking me home?' Vogue asked, wiggling her eyebrows suggestively to get a rise out of Amelia.

'No, I'm dropping you home.'

So she wants to play hard to get. I can cope with that.

Vogue leant her head against the window and closed her eyes.

For now, anyway.

Chapter Eleven

Clutch down, shift, shit! The car stalled as Amelia tried to change the BMW up a gear. She pulled a face as the gears ground and let out an awful noise as it refused to slot into its allotted space. Inwardly cringing, she pressed her foot harder against the clutch and let out a sigh of relief when it easily changed gear. She hadn't driven a manual car in years, and this was no time to practice in one – especially when it was expensive.

Keeping her eyes glued to the road ahead of her as the rain fell rhythmically on the rooftop, she concentrated on the Sat Nav's directions as if her life depended on it. She had absolutely no clue where she was going. Trying to navigate London's roads was not made any easier by the fact that 4x4s were parked either side, making the street even narrower than it would have been normally. To add to an already stressful situation, as much as she wanted to turn and look at Vogue, she daren't. It was intoxicating to be in such close proximity with the woman who she had felt an instant attraction to. What drew her in was her sun-kissed flawless skin, her delicate bone structure and her sensually curved lips, but it was Vogue's eyes that really caught Amelia's attention – where she had lost herself.

She still couldn't figure out how it was even possible to have such a restless feeling gnawing inside her for a woman she had only met once – well twice now.

The yearning, almost a compulsion, had been with her ever since she'd left Vogue's office earlier that day. Since then, she'd been savouring every second of it, replaying it over and over again in her mind's eye. Their encounter had been like a scene from a Hollywood movie, except this was real life, not something made up inside a writer's head.

Perhaps listening to the numerous talks on YouTube about soulmates and twin flames had warped her thought process. There were so many conflicting views on the topic that she didn't know what to believe. Maybe that was the problem, listening to what others experienced instead of trusting her own gut instinct.

'Oops.' Amelia broke suddenly as a cyclist darted out in front of her.

The near collision prompted memories of the accident she'd had earlier that day, and the attraction she felt towards Melissa. *Wow, two women in one day. That's a first!*

All thoughts of Melissa had evaporated when Amelia walked into Vogue's office.

As the Sat Nav signalled for her to turn left, Amelia tried to push the constant thoughts of Vogue aside and concentrate on her driving but didn't succeed. Cecile's warning still unnerved her. As did the unhealthy dynamic of Vogue potentially being her boss.

Essentially, Vogue could make or break her. Maybe Amelia should just ask her there and then whether or not she'd been successful. At least she'd know where she stood.

'I take it you don't normally drive manuals?' Vogue's voice suddenly filled the air.

Roused from her thoughts, a flush crept up Amelia's cheeks. All this time, she'd thought Vogue had been asleep, totally unaware of the haphazard way she was handling her car.

'That obvious huh?' Amelia said as she brushed away a strand of stray hair that fell over her eye, obscuring her vision slightly.

'I'd have to be deaf not to hear the way you're grinding those gears.'

As long as you can't hear what's going on in my mind, I don't care.

'Yeah, sorry about that. I'll get the hang of it in a minute.'

Amelia shot a quick glance at Vogue, thinking she would be looking out of the window but to her shock, Vogue was staring straight at her – unapologetically.

Her palms now clammy, Amelia gripped the steering wheel tightly as her hands were shaking so much. She needed to keep her cool. To not let her emotions get the better of her.

Of course, this was easier said than done.

Her emotions were in overdrive and there was no way of reining them back in.

She slowed the vehicle down and took a sharp right, streetlights illuminating the narrow street.

'If you pull up on the left, that'd be great,' Vogue said, unbuckling her seat belt.

Her breath caught in her throat. Her insides

involuntarily constricting. Amelia was almost in a panic. They'd arrived and she hadn't even realised.

Conflicted because their time together was up so soon, Amelia didn't know what to do next. Make small talk to prolong their time together? No, Vogue didn't look like she was in the mood. Should Amelia escort her to her door in the hope of being asked in for coffee?

No to that too. What would be the point? Besides, Cecile would be wondering where she'd gone if she didn't get back to the bar pretty sharpish. She still hadn't decided whether or not to tell her about driving Vogue home.

If Amelia did, she knew she'd never hear the end of it. Cecile would be convinced Vogue had somehow engineered it in order to get Amelia back to her flat to have her wicked way with her.

If only.

Not that Amelia was up for a one-night stand. In all honesty, she'd never understood the point of them. She had never felt horny enough to sleep with some random woman. Amelia was a talker, so the thought of talking dirty to a stranger filled her with dread.

'Right, well that's you home safely,' Amelia said, unbuckling her own belt before getting out of the car. She didn't trust herself to remain in such close quarters with Vogue.

Seconds later, they both stood on the pavement, facing one another in an awkward silence.

'Thanks,' Vogue said.

'You're welcome.'

Amelia took out her phone and pulled up the Uber app she had downloaded earlier that day. Driving around London in her own car was obviously an accident waiting to happen. She wasn't used to the craziness of people trying to get somewhere fast for absolutely no reason. She had been cut in front of, sworn at, had people roll their eyes at her with that 'women can't drive' look, been hooted at, and nearly run off the road. It was surely a sign from the heavens telling her to leave her car at home. She had no idea how delivery drivers didn't go insane.

'You taking an Uber?' Vogue asked.

Amelia nodded.

'How long?'

'Three minutes.' *And then I'll be out of your company, not knowing when or if I'll ever see you again.*

'Too bad…'

Amelia raised her eyebrows in answer to her comment. Would she be messing with her? Did she actually mean that in some kind of flirty Mills and Boons 'The boss and her employee' way? Though the titles were unfortunate, Amelia had once been addicted to such books. That's probably where she gained such high expectations for her love life. Though saying that, the push and pull games were meant to end with both people in bed having mind-blowing sex. In her case, she just got pushed and that was the end of the story.

If there was one piece of advice Amelia would give to any young woman growing up, it would be to steer clear of romance novels. As far as she was concerned, they should be labelled with health warnings. Better to find out about love the hard way, and Amelia would know about that more than anybody.

'I would've invited you in for a drink,' Vogue said, her eyes dancing mischievously.

There was an energy shift in the atmosphere.

'No disrespect intended but I don't think you need any more alcohol.' *And somehow, I don't think being alone in a room with you is something I need right now.*

'Who was talking about alcohol? Believe it or not, I do have tea and coffee, not to mention soft drinks.'

'I wasn't implying—'

'I should hope not,' Vogue said with a grin. 'I know I mentioned it earlier, but I really am impressed with your designs. I think you're going to go a long way in this industry.'

Amelia's cheeks burned. 'You don't have to say that.'

Vogue took Amelia's hand and squeezed it gently, causing her fingers to prickle, and heat to slowly disperse around her body. *Oh God, why are you punishing me like this?*

'It's true. You're a very talented woman. You've got vision. An eye for what appeals to women.'

Does that include you? The words were at the tip of Amelia's tongue but failed to materialise into actual speech. Her head was in a daze, the effect of Vogue's touch. Instead, she simply said, 'Thanks.'

'You're very humble, aren't you? I like that.'

It wouldn't be the first time someone had mistaken Amelia's low self-esteem for being humble, and if it was anyone bar Vogue, she would have corrected them. But if that's how Vogue wanted to see her, who was she to say anything different?

Amelia could scarcely believe the change in her fortune. Last week, she was desperate to be on anyone's radar, let alone a successful businesswoman's, yet here she was today, being told by Vogue all the things she had longed to hear.

A sudden thought held her mind in a vice type grip. *Don't get too carried away by her compliments. Remember what Cecile warned you about.*

A flash of annoyance caused her to cross her arms tightly around her chest. She wasn't going to let Vogue play her like she had so many other women. Amelia was better than that, or at least she would try to be. London was full of women. Women who would want to be with her and only her.

Amelia was part relieved and part pissed off when a black Mercedes pulled up beside her. She would have enjoyed playing cat and mouse all night with Vogue. And now she was going to have to go back to an empty bed with her head full of fantasies about a woman she had only met hours before.

'Here's my ride,' Amelia said, pulling the car door open and getting inside.

Vogue remained standing by the lamppost, her eyes wide as if in shock.

Amelia smiled triumphantly. This was the first time she had felt an ounce of self-respect. She made a promise to herself that if someone didn't want to be with her and only her, she could do better. She would do better.

Her positive attitude only lasted until the car reached the end of the road. Despite not wanting to turn around and take one last look at Vogue, she couldn't help herself. When she did, her heart sank.

As much as Amelia wanted to, resisting Vogue was going to take all the strength and willpower she had.

At that moment, she had neither.

Chapter Twelve

'Hey, Amelia, so I was wondering… do you fancy going out on a date? *Are you for real – go out on a date? You think this is the 1950s?*

Melissa stepped away from the bathroom mirror and walked back into her bedroom. It didn't matter how many times she practiced her 'speech', it never got any better. In fact, it sounded more juvenile with each attempt. She couldn't believe it had been months since she'd asked someone out for a drink. This was only because Melissa had never met anyone she liked enough. It was mind boggling to think that out of all the millions of people in the world, she struggled to find one person. *Until now that is.*

Whatever the case, Melissa was out of practice and she desperately needed to update her flirting skills.

Melissa thought back to earlier that day and wondered if she'd ever have Vogue's confidence when it came to women. It wasn't that she thought they would reject her. She simply froze when it came to being intimate with another woman, whether emotionally or physically. As soon as Melissa tried to talk, it was as if someone stuffed an invisible cloth in her mouth, rendering her speechless. This made her look awkward, or worse, elusive. Which she was neither. Her parents' way of communicating had obviously rubbed off on her. Neither of them were particularly outgoing nor talkative people, preferring to spend all their free time together, even making Melissa feel as if she were intruding in their little cocoon if she wanted some attention. Inside, she had been side-lined by the two people who were supposed to care for her.

Melissa couldn't ever remember being hugged or told that she was loved by either one of them. They reserved that kind of treatment for each other. The only true affection she got throughout her life was from Peppy, the dog they bought for her when she was eight. A present, she was sure, to occupy her and not bother them.

From the little she knew about Vogue's upbringing; Melissa was certain it wouldn't have been as pitiful as her own. She was probably adored as a baby and treasured through her life as she grew into a teenager.

In her eyes it just wasn't fair.

Aside from the fact that she was drop dead gorgeous, Vogue just had a way with people that seemed to draw them in. It was done with such ease, Melissa couldn't help but think Vogue put people under some kind of magic spell.

She knew it wouldn't be long before Amelia was one of those people, unless she acted first of course. But when? That was the million-dollar question. The poor woman hadn't even been told if she was hired yet and Vogue was already trying to hit on her. *Not hired yet.*

Melissa knew Vogue like the back of her own hand. She was going to hire Amelia all right, but she was going to make her sweat for a while until she told her. She liked to have power over people. Treat them like pawns on a chest board. Always one step ahead. Which made Melissa think that she should forget Amelia and be on the lookout for someone completely new. *Someone that isn't associated with work, or Vogue.*

Yes, that's what she'd do. She'd strike out on her own. Meet someone that Vogue couldn't get her claws into. And when Styles finally closed its doors, she could leave London altogether. Let Vogue live the rest of her life wondering where and why it had all gone wrong.

There was no point sitting around feeling sorry for herself, so Melissa decided to head out to a bar. She wanted to be around people tonight. Even if she didn't speak to anyone, it made her feel less alone.

Within twenty minutes, Melissa was dressed and outside waiting for a taxi. Another ten minutes and she was heading inside BH1. She had no doubt Vogue would have left by then.

Melissa made her way to the bar and ordered herself a double G&T.

'Hey, Mel!'

The voice was familiar. As was the face.

'Cecile, long time no see.' Melissa leant in for a quick embrace. 'How've you been? I haven't seen you around for a while.'

'Been busy, you know how things get in the office. Quiet one minute, manic the next.'

'Yeah, I'll drop by and see you this week'

Cecile was actually one of the few people at Styles Melissa liked. She wasn't fake and pretending to be someone she wasn't.

'Cool. It'll be good to catch up.'

'You here alone?'

'No, I'm with my friend,' Cecile said. 'She's in London for a couple of days so I thought I'd show her around.'

Cecile took a mouthful of beer, placing her other hand on a bar stool to balance herself.

'Maybe you should swap that for water,' Melissa said, gesturing to her bottle. Clearly, she'd had one too many.

Cecile laughed. 'Where's the fun in that?'

'There you are, I thought you'd left.' The voice caught Melissa off guard. 'Melissa?'

Melissa turned to look straight into Amelia's eyes. Like a kid let loose in a sweet shop with no restraints, Melissa felt like all her Christmases had come at once. She had hoped to see Amelia again but never dreamt it would be so soon.

'Amelia.'

Amelia smiled at her, genuinely pleased to see her, and Melissa smiled back, feeling a warmth engulf her.

'Is this the local hangout for you guys from Styles?' Amelia asked.

Melissa looked at her questioningly.

'Vogue was in here earlier.'

And she went home without you? Now that's a positive sign. Maybe I've got it all wrong about Vogue. Some people can withstand her charm.

'Yeah, she said she'd drop by, it's the nearest bar to the office so we all tend to gravitate here,' Melissa said, before suddenly making the connection between Amelia and Cecile. 'Hang on, are you two friends?'

'Yes,' Amelia said looking at Cecile fondly.

'Well, let me buy you a drink,' Melissa said. The fact that they were friends elevated Amelia even more in her estimation. If Cecile vouched for her, she was obviously a good person.

'I'll leave you two to get on then, I'm going for a boogie,' Cecile said, grabbing the woman next to her and pulling her towards the small dance floor.

Melissa couldn't believe her luck. What was the likelihood of bumping into Amelia in a bar? The night was still young, so there was plenty of time for them to get to know each other on a more personal level.

'So, what're you drinking?' Melissa said, raising her hand to catch the barwoman's attention.

'A coke please.'

'Coke?' Melissa tried to hide the disappointment in her voice. It wasn't that she wanted to get Amelia drunk. Far from it. She just wanted to have a relaxed atmosphere between them, where they could both lower their guards, take off their social masks and show each other the real person. That was the problem these days, everyone had a façade that wasn't even close to who they really were. It was both frustrating and annoying that half the time she didn't know who she was relating to – the person themselves or their alter ego.

Amelia slid onto the vacant stool next to her while she ordered her drink.

'I can't believe Cecile's your friend,' Melissa said

once she'd been served.

'Me neither. She is such an amazing woman. A true inspiration.' Amelia took a sip of her drink. 'I can't imagine what my life would be like without her.'

'It must be nice having such a good friend.'

Amelia laughed. 'Oh, believe me, we aren't that perfect. We have our moments.'

'Fighting over boyfriends I take it?' Melissa said in order to test the waters.

'Oh no, I'm gay,' Amelia replied.

Before Melissa could respond, a man came from behind Amelia and tapped her shoulder.

'You here with the bird who was imitating John Travolta on the dance floor?'

Amelia turned to face the man. 'Yeah, why?'

'You'd better go help her. My missus said she's in the toilets throwing up. You'd think a woman of her age would know better.'

Melissa was just about to retort with a sarcastic comment, but Amelia put a reassuring hand on her knee before she got to her feet.

'Ignore him. Well, thanks for the drink. I suppose I'd better take her home.'

And then she was gone. Weaving her way through people as she headed in the direction of the toilets.

Melissa remained sitting there, completely dumbfounded. She'd had the opportunity of a lifetime right in her hands and then it vanished. Puff. Just like that.

All their encounter had served to do was prove to her that she wasn't meant to be with anyone else. That fate had other plans for her and Amelia. After all, why else would fate have placed Amelia here tonight when Melissa could have met anyone else.

If it was meant to be, it was meant to be.

Melissa decided to let things pan out all by themselves.

Chapter Thirteen

Amelia finally managed to get Cecile settled into bed, but only after Cecile had thrown up the entire contents of her stomach which there seemed to be no end of. How Amelia hadn't joined her over the toilet bowl was a miracle. Just the smell alone of regurgitated beer and the prawn curry they'd eaten earlier was enough to induce Amelia's gag reflex.

It was a good thing Amelia could hold her breath for a long time. She lasted two minutes before her heart felt like it was going to explode. Then it was a quick intake of fresh air out of the window then back to the job at hand – making sure Cecile didn't vomit on her hair in the toilet bowl, by keeping it held back out of her face.

It was strange. In all the time Amelia had known Cecile, she'd never seen her in such a state. Amelia knew Cecile was a party girl, but she was never out of control. In fact, she couldn't actually recall ever really seeing her drunk before. Tipsy, yes, but never like this.

Amelia dropped two tablets of Alka-Seltzer into a large glass of water and held the back of Cecile's limp head as she tried to coax her lips to the rim. It was a feat in itself, as Cecile was insistent on communicating with Amelia via long groans and barely audible declarations of never touching alcohol again. Despite this, Cecile managed to empty the contents of the glass. Amelia managed to get her into bed and she finally dropped off to sleep laying on her side. Leaving a bucket beside the bed, just in case her stomach found something more to discard, Amelia switched off the lamp and gave Cecile a quick peck on the cheek.

Amelia closed the bedroom door gently behind her and made her way back to her own room. Quickly undressing, she laid her clothes on the wicker chair in the corner and slipped between the cool white sheets. Casting a glance over at the bedside clock, Amelia groaned when she saw how late it was – three a.m. – under four hours left to catch up on some sleep.

The likelihood of that happening was close to zero. Now Cecile was no longer her main concern, her thoughts returned to Vogue… and Melissa. It was strange how she felt within the brief time that she'd spent with each of them. With Vogue, her attraction was undeniable – that much was obvious – but when it came to Melissa, she made Amelia feel like she was surrounded in cotton wool. She was more like the protector rather than the hunter, which Vogue obviously was.

Amelia wasn't one hundred percent sure, but the way Melissa had looked at her earlier made her believe she either fancied her or just liked her a lot. Amelia hoped it was the latter because although she found her very attractive, the spark she'd had with Vogue just wasn't there between them.

Taking her phone from the bedside cabinet, Amelia set the alarm for six, just to be on the safe side. Her appointment with an up and coming new design house in Covent Garden was at eight o'clock, and she didn't want to oversleep. It was just in case she didn't get the trainee position at Styles. If being in London for only one day had taught her anything, it was that this was the place to be if she wanted to get noticed.

Just as she was about to put her phone back down, the email icon popped up on her screen and she absentmindedly pressed it, expecting to see junk mail. What she hadn't expected was an email from Vogue. Amelia blinked several times as she tried to take the words in.

She had been chosen to be a trainee.

This is it!

The moment she had been waiting for all her life. The opportunity to show the world what she had to offer. Not to mention getting to work with some of the most talented people in the industry. Amelia could only imagine what kind of doors would be open to her from now on. Both professionally and personally.

And she would be working with Vogue! Amelia didn't know which prospect excited her most out of the two.

Now her position was confirmed, Amelia had to get her act together and sort out her move to London, that meant she had to give notice to her landlord for her flat. *That's going to be fun… not.* She'd only moved in six months previously and had promised that she would stay for at least two years. At the time, that had been her plan as she had applied for the trainee position at Styles but had not heard back from them, so wrongly assumed it was a rejection. She just hoped Roger was kind and understanding when she told him the news.

Too excited to sleep now, Amelia had to cancel the meeting arranged in the morning. Grabbing her laptop from the floor, she flipped the lid open and fired off an email to apologise for any inconvenience she may have caused.

Once that was out of the way, she went back to daydreaming about the woman who had been occupying her mind ever since Amelia had laid eyes on her. Even though she was now officially her boss, fantasising about her wasn't stepping over anyone's boundaries. It wasn't as if Vogue was going to have access to her mind and see all the naughty things that resided there.

She'd have to hide her feelings from now on. Anything to do with Vogue was going to have to be done covertly, and this is where she was thankful for Instagram. The perfect platform for her to set up her stalker nest.

Amelia logged into Instagram and typed in Vogue's name, then waited for her profile to load.

Oh how I wish I hadn't looked now. Why did I look?

Amelia tried her hardest not to allow herself to become triggered by jealousy as she took in images of Vogue posing with some of the most beautiful women she had ever seen. In that moment, Amelia realised how stupid she had been. Naive. To have thought for even a nanosecond that someone like Vogue would be interested in her, just went to show how disconnected from reality she was.

Don't look, don't look, don't look, she repeated like a mantra as she tore her eyes away from Vogue's smiling face. Hadn't she learnt anything from how crap social media made her feel in general, just by looking at strangers' posts. What did she think was going to happen spying on someone she had met in real life and who she really, really, liked? She had no one to blame but herself for feeling in the depths of despair. If she had remained ignorant to the reality of Vogue's life, she could have played make-believe that the chemistry she imagined they had was actually real. That Vogue actually felt it too. Instead, she would have to come to terms with the fact that, yet again, she was in want of something she could never have.

Filled with disappointment, Amelia made a promise to herself that she would not, under any circumstances, look at Vogue's Instagram profile again or any of her social media pages for that matter. Unless she wanted to torture herself that was.

How could she have been so stupid to have believed, even for a moment, that what she thought was an attraction, was nothing more than her mind playing tricks on her.

There was no point her overanalysing things. Misreading women's intentions seemed to be the story of her life. This was just another setback that she would have to get used to, like she always did.

Her thoughts now swapped to Melissa. Had she misread her body language as well?

Surely not. Amelia had noticed the way Melissa's gaze had roamed over her face, slowly, longingly. Not to mention the intense stare that was normally reserved for something or someone people particularly liked the look of.

So if it was the case Melissa was attracted to her, would that be enough to try and erase Vogue from her thoughts? As much as she'd like to believe so, Amelia knew it wasn't the case. There was something about Vogue that had reeled her in, and she was still there, thrashing around at the end of her line.

If I feel like this now, what will it be like when, or if, I get to know her better?

There was only one solution to this, Amelia reasoned.

It's easy, just don't get to know her.

Why did she feel a tug of despair in her heart at the very thought of it?

Chapter Fourteen

Vogue was relieved when the very last interviewee walked out of the conference room and quietly shut the door behind her. Interviewing people was her least favourite thing in the world. Though she was fine when it came to making business decisions, having to reject twelve out of the fifteen people that had sat in front of her, was something she could have done without.

Vogue took a mouthful of water before turning to Melissa who was looking as vacant as she felt. It had been a tiring few hours.

'Well, what did you think?'

'Definitely not Poppy,' Melissa said, referring to the woman that had just left. 'I don't think she answered one of your questions directly.'

Vogue picked up the woman's CV. 'I think it was just nerves. Didn't you see the way her hands trembled when she held the glass?'

Vogue put the CV aside and took hold of a pile of folders that contained the other thirteen applicants. One spot had already been filled by Amelia. Vogue had known the second she'd laid eyes on her that she would hire her. Not necessarily because of the magnetic draw to her. It was more than that. Vogue really did think she possessed a unique talent.

'So three to choose from all of these,' Vogue said, exhaling a deep breath.

'Let me order a takeaway,' Melissa said, taking her

phone from her pocket. 'I think it's going to be a late one.'

'I agree.' Vogue glanced at her watch and realised she hadn't eaten since morning.

An hour later, after consuming most of a pepperoni pizza and three cups of coffee, they were ready to whittle down the fifteen to three.

'So what did you think of Sarah?' Melissa asked.

Vogue looked thoughtful as she leafed through Sarah's CV. She remembered the perky blonde-haired woman as being very ambitious. Perhaps too ambitious for the role Vogue was offering. She wanted a team player, whereas Sarah struck her as someone who would leave you hanging out to dry if a better opportunity arose. This was so against Vogue's values as loyalty was a top priority. So it was with this in mind, Vogue shook her head and put her CV to the side.

'I agree,' Melissa said. 'She looks the type that would sell her own mother if it meant getting ahead.'

Vogue laughed. 'My thoughts exactly.'

'People like that scare me. Not that being ambitious isn't a good thing but the fact that everything else falls by the wayside in order for them to reach a goal. That takes a different kind of person.'

'Exactly and most definitely not the kind that would fit in here. The last thing I need is to keep looking over my shoulder.'

'Yeah and to be honest, I wasn't that impressed with her portfolio. Something about it was lacking,' Melissa said.

'Plus, her vision seems to be focused on being at the top, not how she's going to get there.'

'So she's a no then,' Melissa said with finality. 'Okay, how about Trudy? I liked her.'

'Me too,' Vogue said in reference to the bespectacled, petite woman. She had impressed Vogue with her knowledge of the fashion industry. She knew every design house in London, the latest collections and who was in and who was out.

'Her designs are refreshing and well thought-out. They're not just about looking good, she also factors in the suitability of the garments. But do you think her style can ever reach the X factor?' Melissa asked.

'That, I don't know. Let's put her on the maybe pile.'

Melissa nodded in agreement.

'Right, next up, Jordan.'

Melissa perked up at her name and Vogue could understand why. It seemed they both had been taken with her. In her early thirties, Jordan had walked into the interview with the confidence of Muhammad Ali in a boxing ring, and her talent backed her up. Elegant, sleek designs which would appeal to the woman that wanted that extra touch without looking ridiculous. Vogue had lost count of the amount of times she had been at a fashion show and the clothes the models had walked down the catwalk in had rendered her speechless. Until this day, she never knew where the women who bought the ridiculous outfits actually wore them. After a healthy dose of buyer's remorse, they were probably shoved into the back of a wardrobe, never to be seen again.

'I think it's a given that she should come on-board,' Melissa said. 'I think she was the best out of all of them.'

'I agree, next is….'

Vogue pulled out another file and for the next couple of hours they debated the pros and cons of each applicant until they finally had the three they were looking for. Jordan, Trudy and Naomi, a woman straight out of University who had shown some talent already.

'Well, that wasn't as bad as I thought,' Vogue said, pushing herself to her feet. The relief was overwhelming that they could now move on with trying to save the company. Having been initially disappointed by the applications, Vogue had been pleasantly surprised by a few of the interviewees.

'Nope. So, you got plans for tonight?'

'Yes, a sleeping tablet and a good audiobook,' Vogue said.

'Good, you look like you need the rest,' Melissa said, slipping into her jacket.

'I'd normally take that as an insult, but I've seen myself in the mirror and I totally agree.'

The women shared a brief smile then went their separate ways.

Chapter Fifteen

Vogue arrived an hour earlier than she normally would, but it was the trainees' first day and she wanted to make sure she was there on their arrival. Then they could get straight down to business. It would be the first time she'd seen Amelia again since the interview. During that time, she hadn't been far from Vogue's thoughts and now, even thinking her name unleashed a tremor of desire within.

As much as Vogue tried to ignore the effect Amelia had on her, the feelings only intensified the more she tried to push them away. Somehow, for reasons totally unknown to her, Amelia had got under her skin, in a way no stranger ever had.

Smiling as she read a funny meme on her phone Carol had sent her, Vogue didn't realise anyone else was in the office until she looked up and came face-to-face with Amelia.

Her smile faltered as she came to an abrupt standstill. Powerless to move. Incapable of uttering a single syllable, Vogue's world tilted on its axis. All she could do was stare at her. Vogue could only imagine the impression she was giving.

'Sorry, I didn't mean to startle you,' Amelia said, breaking the silence.

I'm giving the impression of being startled apparently. She'd go with that. As long as it wasn't that of a lovesick teenager.

'I was miles away.' Vogue finally found her voice.

Amelia's lips curved in amusement. 'I could tell.'

Vogue's stomach constricted. Coming in early was a terrible mistake. She should have made sure Melissa was there as back up, just in case. Being one-to-one with Amelia was not something she had expected, nor felt she could cope with at this moment in time.

Amelia still held her gaze. Was she challenging her? Did she know her presence was holding her heart captive?

Get a grip! You're in charge. Say something. Do something.

Vogue's emotions were holding her hostage. She prayed for divine intervention. That someone would come in, even if it was a cleaner, but it was to no avail. Nobody was coming to rescue her.

The awkwardness of the moment now filled the room and even Amelia looked a little unsettled at Vogue's lack of interaction.

'So have I got a desk?' Amelia said, gesturing to the four desks adjacent to each other.

Vogue followed her gaze, thankful for the distraction. It was all she needed to get back in control of her faculties.

'Yes,' Vogue said, swallowing the lump in her throat. 'But I'll let you into a secret. The one at the end's better. You'll get a great view of the park from there.'

Amelia smiled sending her heart racing, all the while standing there looking as cool as a cucumber. Either Amelia couldn't feel the chemistry in the air, or she was a very good actor. *She'd make a great poker player either way.*

Running her finger along the top of the desk, Amelia said, 'I really appreciate being given the opportunity to work here you know.'

Vogue was entranced with the way Amelia's finger glided gracefully along the desktop, momentarily wondering what it would feel like running over her own naked skin.

'I'm glad to have you on-board,' Vogue said, her voice unintentionally dropping an octave, making it sound husky and seductive.

Amelia raised her eyebrows and Vogue forced herself to hold her gaze, despite the playful twinkle in her eyes. Vogue couldn't afford to let Amelia get to her like this. She had to stamp her authority on the situation before it got out of hand.

Vogue tightly clasped her fingers together. Partly because they were actually trembling and partly because she didn't know what to do with them.

'Well, get yourself settled. The kitchen's just over there if you need anything. I'll get Melissa to come in and give you all a briefing. I've got to get ready for a meeting,' Vogue said, not quite understanding why she felt the need to explain herself.

As Vogue made her way to her office, the sensation in her chest made her feel like cupid's arrow had landed right bang in the middle of her heart.

***

Whoa that was tense! Vogue had looked as shocked as Amelia felt when she walked in unexpectedly. Amelia had arrived early to familiarise herself with her workspace. She hated having to ask busy people for help as a newbie, so to take the sting out of the first day, whenever she started anywhere new, she would find out where everything was. If Amelia would have known Vogue was going to be there, she wasn't sure she'd have been so fast. Despite the loudness of her heartbeat pounding in her ears, she was mightily pleased with herself for doing such a good job at keeping her emotions under control.

Amelia managed to keep her voice neutral which was odd as that was normally the first tell-tale sign of her nervousness. She had also managed to maintain eye contact with Vogue which had been the most difficult. Sultry came to mind when she racked her brain for a description of Vogue's eyes. Amelia hadn't failed to notice her cleavage either, though she'd tried her hardest to keep her eyes directly above Vogue's chin. Anywhere else would have proved very dangerous.

Amelia exhaled a long breath as she put her bag on her desk and turned to look out of the window at the view Vogue mentioned. She was right. Opposite was a park with large oak trees and a medium-sized lake. Mothers with their children were standing at the edge, throwing food to the many ducks that lined up in front of them.

As Amelia sat down at her desk, she couldn't help but wonder what it was going to be like working for Vogue. How would she cope seeing her every day with a mammoth crush on her? Amelia only hoped it wouldn't interfere with her concentration. It was bad enough already trying to go five minutes without Vogue's face popping up in her mind's eye.

All Amelia had to do was keep reminding herself that Vogue was a guilty pleasure and what went on in her mind, stayed in her mind.

That wouldn't be so hard to do, would it?

Chapter Sixteen

Vogue sat at her desk, head back, eyes closed, when she heard Melissa's voice.

'You still having problems sleeping?'

Vogue opened her eyes.

'Yeah, some nights are better than others.'

Truth was, it was more than just a problem with sleeping, the past week had been one of such stress, Vogue had no idea how she was still functioning. When she wasn't thinking about Amelia, she was trying to conjure up plans to put her business back together. Her success rate so far seemed to be stuck on zero.

'So, are you ready?' Melissa asked as she flicked through a file she had brought in with her.

'For the meeting with the bank?' Vogue asked.

Melissa nodded. 'D'you want me to come with you?'

'Yes.' Vogue picked up a pencil and tapped it repeatedly against the edge of her desk, her emotions still feeling out of sync. 'I still can't believe I got us into this mess.'

'You've got to stop blaming yourself,' Melissa said, snapping her files shut.

'Who else is there to blame?'

'How about the actual person that's responsible.'

'I'm in charge, Mel, me, not anyone else. I should've noticed something was amiss but was too busy. I took my eye off the ball—'

'Vogue, you're being way too hard on yourself. You had a lot to deal with. To be honest, I don't know where you got the strength from. If it was me, I would've buckled under the weight of it all.'

'It's irrelevant now. It is what it is. The company needs money and I've got to somehow come up with it.'

It was hard to believe that barely a year ago, Vogue had the world at her feet.

The rich and famous were clamouring at her door to be the first one to be dressed by Styles for an award ceremony. She was the cream of the crop. Each day was a challenge. Exciting, exhilarating, as Vogue and her team fought to keep their competitors at bay by creating stylish fashionwear that could make anybody look a million dollars. They were riding a crest, one they thought would keep going until one day it didn't.

Her mother found a lump in her breast.

Six months later, Vogue stood by her coffin.

A month later, she had been told the devastating news that Bev's secret was going to be exposed. Not only had she lost her mother, but after the pay-out, most of her money was gone.

Completely lost, Vogue had hit rock bottom and did something she'd never done before.

She buried her head in the sand. Refused to acknowledge the reality of what her life had become.

Eventually, it was the wisdom of a simple sentence that finally brought her back from the edge. That gave her the courage to fight on, 'Though one chapter is finished, it doesn't mean your story is over.'

If it wasn't for that, there would have been no reason for Vogue to go on. To fight for the company she had built from scratch. To fight for her life.

Once she was back on her feet, even Bev's betrayal was not enough to stop her momentum from trying to get back on top.

A knock at the door caused Vogue and Melissa to look in its direction.

'Come in,' Vogue called out.

The door slowly opened, then Amelia's head appeared through the crack, a nervous smile on her lips as she walked into the room, arms clasped behind her back.

Vogue straightened in her seat, the very sight of Amelia flustering her.

'Am I interrupting anything?'

'No, of course not, come, sit down,' Vogue said, her voice cautiously calm despite the eruption going on inside.

Amelia brought her hands around to her front and it was then Vogue saw the folder she held in her hand. Vogue couldn't take her eyes off Amelia as she made her way across the room and took a seat, giving Melissa a nod of acknowledgement in the process.

The three women sat in an uncomfortable silence. Vogue's brain was vacant. She simply couldn't piece a sentence together. Instead, she just sat there praying Melissa would take the initiative and speak. But she didn't which left it down to Amelia.

'I wanted to show you something, if that's okay.'

Vogue nodded, not trusting herself to speak. She cursed her body's response as butterflies swarmed aimlessly around and around in her stomach.

As unbelievable as it sounded, Vogue had never experienced anything like this before. She would have laughed had it not been such an inappropriate moment.

'I apologise in advance if I'm getting ahead of myself, but since you liked the designs I showed you before, I thought you might be interested in ones that are in the same vein.'

That's what I call initiative. Now Amelia had her full attention and it was no longer an attraction. It was pure business.

It had been a long time since someone had walked into Vogue's office and impressed her with their attitude.

'I'd be very interested,' Vogue said, barely able to hide the excitement in her voice.

If Amelia was as good as she thought, Vogue knew they were onto a winner.

One by one, Amelia brought out A3 sheets of paper. With each design, Vogue's mouth opened just that little bit wider as she studied them in depth. The craftsmanship of the jackets and coats were a combination of modern and traditional styles. A balance of both style and functionality.

The woman had talent. Pizazz. Amelia had… IT! That special something that made a design stand out from the rest, and thankfully, she was on Vogue's team.

After a long moment of stunned silence, Vogue

finally found her voice.

'Do you have any idea about the materials—'

Amelia nodded. 'All sustainable. I thought it might be a good idea to do an eco-friendly collection. It seems to be the in thing nowadays.'

Vogue looked up, straight into Amelia's eyes and hoped she would be able to read the gratitude in her expression.

Amelia turned to Melissa. 'What do you think?'

'It's not Melissa you need to impress,' Vogue said before Melissa had a chance to speak.

As much as she respected Melissa as her PA, this was her call.

Vogue didn't fail to notice a look of disappointment in Amelia's eyes. Was it because she thought Vogue wasn't a team player? That, of course, was the furthest thing from the truth. Normally, she thrived on her colleagues' input. *Normally*. But now wasn't the time to open up the forum for others' opinions. She needed to make the right choice. It was up to her to save the company. Her and her alone.

Vogue glanced down at the sketches again.

And maybe Amelia.

Chapter Seventeen

A third wheel. That was the only description Melissa could use to explain how she'd felt during the meeting that had just taken place. A third wheel that had absolutely no use. Vogue had totally undermined her position in front of a complete stranger, and it was downright embarrassing. 'Melissa's not the one that needs impressing,' she mimicked.

Melissa exhaled a pent-up breath in a long sigh. So it was perfectly okay for Vogue to rely on her opinion for almost everything, except when it came to having her say on a collection design? If that was the case, why had Melissa even bothered to be present at the interviews if she wasn't the one that had to be impressed?

What the hell was Vogue thinking?

That's just it. She obviously wasn't thinking. No, that was a lie, she was thinking but just about someone else.

Melissa could tell a mile off, from Vogue's body language, she had the hots for Amelia – bad. But this was the first time she had seen Vogue visibly fight against her emotions. Melissa had known her long enough to be able to read the signs.

She'd been tense, as if she was afraid. But afraid of what? Her feelings… for Amelia? *No way!*

As attractive and talented as Amelia was, she just couldn't see Vogue falling hard for someone with her temperament. Sleep with her, yes. A long term prospect?

She didn't think so. Vogue liked a woman that challenged her in every sense. Someone elusive, who played hard to get. She also liked successful women. No disrespect to Amelia, but she was just starting out and the two women were leagues apart. The balance of power heavily weighted in Vogue's favour. *For now anyway…. Right, time for me to focus.*

Melissa had to start the ball rolling on her plan to bring down Styles once and for all, and it wasn't going to get done anytime soon if she sat there daydreaming about Amelia and Vogue. That situation would work itself out once the doors to Styles were finally closed.

She'd already planned phase two. Phase one had worked like a dream. To destabilise Vogue's financial position. Knowing how much Vogue's brand meant to her, Melissa knew that there wasn't a chance in hell she would let Bev's deception go public. She wouldn't have been able to face the humiliation. Melissa had made a good show of trying to convince Vogue not to pay off the student. It really was a win-win for her. If Vogue paid, she'd go bankrupt. If she didn't, she'd lose her reputation and go bankrupt anyway.

By the looks of things, Amelia's designs would have been a huge success, just the thing to put Styles back on the map. It was because of this, Melissa knew she had to move fast and be one step ahead of Vogue, as this unexpected hiccup had caught her off guard.

Most talented designers were snapped up as soon as they left university or showed any sign of originality. Melissa thought Styles would have been inundated with mediocre designers who held the belief they were better than they actually were. She seriously hadn't expected someone with Amelia's talent to slip through the cracks and come on-board

As much as she hated sabotaging Amelia's chance of having her own collection made available to the public, Melissa was sure once she made a few phone calls, she'd have no problem arranging for Amelia to start work at another design house.

But for now, Melissa had to follow through with her plan and couldn't afford to let anyone get in her way. Not even Amelia.

Melissa scrolled down on her phone screen until she found the number she was looking for and pressed it, waiting a few seconds before it was answered.

'Hey, Tina, how's it going?' Melissa tried to sound jovial but even she could hear the insincerity in her own voice, the lack of enthusiasm that came with having to crawl up people's arses. This was one aspect of her life that she wasn't going to miss when she was no longer Vogue's personal 'skivvy' assistant.

'All's good. Listen you're gonna have to make it quick, Melissa, I'm on my way out the door.'

Yeah, like that makes a difference when you're using a mobile phone. A mobile phone Melissa knew was never far away from Tina's ear, even in bed.

'Okay, no probs. So I know you've spoken to Vogue in helping out with the new outwear collection she's working on.'

'Yeah,' Tina said, sounding totally disinterested.

'Can I assume what I tell you will be in the strictest of confidence?'

She could just envision Tina at the other end of the phone, her ears pricking up at the sound of impending gossip.

'Of course. You know me.'

Yes, Melissa knew Tina all right. As soon as she shared with her the news that would bring Styles down, Tina would spread the word like wildfire. And it was for that reason, Melissa wasn't going to spill the beans just yet.

'I can't tell you everything at the moment, but you need to hold off from signing any kind of contract with Vogue.'

'Why? What's going on?'

'Will you just trust me on this? It will save you a lot of trouble in the long run.'

'And what am I supposed to tell Vogue when she wants to discuss things?'

'Make an excuse,' Melissa said, just stopping herself from adding, 'After all, you're good at that.'

It wasn't fair to hold a grudge against Tina, knowing it was her own doing that had led to the demise of their very short-lived romance. Yes, Melissa knew she was mostly to blame, as being emotionally available to her was something she could never quite grasp. Whether that was because she just wasn't into her, she didn't know, but there was something that made her clam up when things started to get a little too comfortable between them. Especially when Tina would 'accidentally' leave items of clothing behind, followed by her toothbrush. It was when Tina wanted to spend every weekend together that Melissa pulled up the drawbridge and drew a line in their relationship. Tina didn't officially dump Melissa, instead, she came out with a whole slew of excuses as to why they couldn't meet for drinks or dinner and it soon fizzled out.

Tina responded with a long-elongated sigh. A sign that she was going to heed her warning.

'Okay, but this better be worth it, Melissa. If we miss out on showing Vogue's collection for nothing, I'm not going to be happy.'

'Trust me on this, you're going to be thanking me on your knees.'

'That's one road I won't be going down again,' Tina quipped.

Before Melissa could respond, Tina hung up.

Melissa grabbed her bag and made her way to Vogue's office, her earlier resentment fading as she looked forward to what the bank had to say about Vogue's need for a loan to save her ailing business.

Chapter Eighteen

'This is a nice treat,' Amelia said before taking a bite out of her spicy hot deep pan pizza. 'On payday, it's my turn.'

'Amelia, you know I don't give to get.'

'I know, but I want to thank you for everything you've done for me. If it wasn't for you, none of this would be happening.' *And I wouldn't have met Vogue.*

Whether that would prove to be a good thing or not remained to be seen, but ever since she'd started at Styles, Amelia had never been more eager to get into work in her life. Neither had she needed to take so many toilet breaks, not because she had a weak bladder but more to do with the fact it entailed passing by Vogue's office.

Just getting sweeping glances of her several times a day was a good enough fix for what now felt like an addiction. Amelia literally couldn't get Vogue out of her head.

Even now, sitting in the relaxed atmosphere of the restaurant, Amelia should be totally present, but she wasn't. She was thinking about the kind of pizza Vogue would have chosen. Whether she would have liked the quaint surroundings or would she have preferred something more upmarket. Her thoughts went around and around on a loop, only stopping when she went to sleep. Only to start again as soon as she woke up.

Amelia had become worried and thought she was

heading for some sort of breakdown, but thanks to Google, she'd found she was suffering from limerence. Now Amelia knew she wasn't going insane, yet anyway, she didn't see the harm in indulging further.

'How're you getting on with your new colleagues?' Cecile asked, sipping her Coke through a straw.

'Yeah, they seem nice enough.'

'Are they any good?'

'I wouldn't know. They pretty much keep to themselves.'

'If you feel like having a chat you can come to my office.'

Amelia squeezed Cecile's hand. 'Thanks but it's fine, I actually get more work done not having to make small talk with them.'

'That's good.'

Looking across the table at Cecile, Amelia suspended her thoughts on Vogue for a moment as she realised Cecile wasn't being her usual self. In fact, she'd been far from normal since Amelia arrived. There was something unspoken in the air between them that she hadn't noticed before.

'Can I ask you a question?' Amelia put her pizza down.

'Sure.'

'And I want you to be totally honest with me.'

'When aren't I?'

Amelia paused for a moment wanting to say the right words, so her true intention wasn't lost. 'Is everything okay between us?'

Cecile frowned. 'Why wouldn't it be?'

'I dunno. I mean if I've overstayed my welcome, you'd tell me, wouldn't you?'

'You haven't overstayed your welcome, Amelia. You can stay as long as you like. You know that.'

'Okay, that's good to know.'

Cecile glanced around their surroundings and Amelia could tell there was something still on her mind. If it wasn't Amelia invading her space, what the hell was it?

It didn't take her long to find out.

'So… has Vogue made a move on you yet?'

Bingo!

Cecile still had an obsession with Vogue. Up until now, Vogue had been nothing but professional and Amelia was still waiting to see a side of her that could explain Cecile's obvious disdain for her.

It was because of this that Amelia kept her interactions with Vogue to herself. So she said nothing, and that was how things were going to be from now on.

Chapter Nineteen

Vogue stood aside to let an elderly woman pass her by before entering the bank. She discreetly wiped her clammy hands on the back of her jeans as she led the way to the customer service desk, giving her details to the woman whose name tag read 'Janet'.

'Take a seat. He won't be long.'

Vogue gave her a tense smile and backed away to a small seating area where she remained standing. She was too on edge to stay in one place and would only start fidgeting if she sat down, which wasn't the image she wanted to portray. She wanted to appear in charge. A woman in control of her own destiny. How was it going to instil a belief of self-confidence if she came across as a nervous wreck? Melissa on the other hand, looked at peace as she sat down and removed a magazine from the glass coffee table. As she flicked through it, totally oblivious to the turmoil Vogue was experiencing, Vogue wondered what she would have done this past year if Melissa hadn't come into her life. Though she had never told her, Melissa truly was her rock. The dependable person that had remained by her side throughout all of the trials and tribulations the last year had thrown at her.

Vogue thanked her lucky stars for being so fortunate. To find Amelia too was an added bonus. If she could persuade the manager to give her a loan, she would finally be on the up and up.

'Do you want some water?' Melissa suddenly said, referring to the water cooler in the corner of the room.

'No. I'm fine,' Vogue replied, clearing her throat. Even though her mouth was as dry as a desert, she didn't think she could swallow anything without bringing it up again. All she wanted was for this meeting to be over and done with. To know where things stood so she could start to put her plans into action.

Just then, Janet gestured for them to come over with a wave of her hand as she hung up the phone. As they neared, the bank manager, James, appeared from a side door. Dressed in a black pinstriped suit, he looked every inch the money man. The man who held Vogue's fate in his hands.

'Vogue, nice to see you,' James said, holding out his hand.

'You too, John.' Vogue gave him a firm handshake. 'You remember Melissa.'

'Of course,' James said, extending his hand to Melissa next. 'Come through to my office.'

James showed them into a colourless, uninspiring room, Vogue was all too familiar with. How many times had she passed through those doors with high expectations for the future? And how many times had she been welcomed with zeal? Plenty. But on this occasion, the energy in the air felt all wrong. There was no buzz of excitement or anticipation for her future projects.

Even before John opened his mouth to tell her the bank's decision, she knew what the answer was going to be. An emphatic no, and she was right.

'I totally understand your predicament, I really do, Vogue, but like I keep telling you, my hands are tied.' James took a seat behind his desk, motioning for them to do the same.

Vogue ran her hands through her hair.

His excuse was a cop out. She knew it and James knew it. He just didn't have the balls to say he didn't think her company was worth the risk anymore, despite all the millions that had been through the bank.

'This is my last chance, James. Some of the major retailers are going to be attending Milan's show. Not to mention the best distributors in the world. It's just the kind of exposure we need to put us back on top. If my collection isn't shown, my business is dead in the water.'

James' expression signalled that those were his exact thoughts. 'I don't know what else to tell you.'

'Come on, there must be something I can do? Anything?' It was humiliating for Vogue to be begging for help, but she had no pride left at this point. It wasn't all about her, she had a team whose livelihoods depended on her. She couldn't, wouldn't let them down.

'Okay, how about I,' Vogue paused for a moment. She couldn't believe she was about to do this but what choice was there? 'use my house as a guarantee.'

James raised his eyebrows, a cloud of alarm sweeping over his features. 'Vogue, you can't mean that.'

'I can and I do.'

'I know how much that house means to you. It was

your mother's—'

'I know who it belonged to.' Vogue snapped before immediately apologising. 'I'm sorry. Look, if that's the only way I can raise the money, it's what I'm going to have to do.'

James opened a file on his desk and shifted the papers around. 'I can offer you a high risk, short term loan to cover the costs for your collection. But you know how this works, if you don't repay the money back in six months, you'll lose your house.'

'I know.'

James averted his gaze momentarily. 'And you're absolutely sure?'

Vogue nodded.

James looked over at Melissa who had remained quiet throughout the entire meeting. 'Okay.'

James turned his attention to his computer and started tapping away on his keyboard. 'I just need you to sign this.'

James tapped one last key before the printer chugged out paper from the other side of the room. He stood and went to retrieve it, scanning the pages as he walked back over to his desk and laid the sheets of paper side by side.

'Do you want to have a read of this first? Take them home and make a decision then?'

Vogue's heart was in her mouth as she looked down at the forms she needed to sign. The enormity of what she was committing herself to hit her full force. Although it was high risk, Vogue knew in her gut it was worth it. Her mother would have been wholeheartedly behind her decision to use the house as collateral, after all, she would always say, 'it's just a house – bricks and mortar, it'll still be here when I'm dead and gone.'

But that didn't mean Vogue wasn't scared. No, scared was an understatement, she was petrified. Everything was dependent on this one gamble now. If she messed this up, she would be left with nothing. No business. No home. No dignity. Nothing.

Then I'd better make sure I succeed.

Vogue leant over the table and silently read the conditions of the loan. Once she was satisfied there wasn't anything amiss, she looked up at James.

'Where's the pen?'

Pursed lips, James reached inside his jacket and handed her one.

Ten minutes later, the women sat side by side in a bar opposite the bank.

Vogue was on her second glass of wine, Melissa still on her first. Despite the alcohol in her system, it did nothing to temper the anxiety she still felt. Though she wasn't one to normally double guess herself, she had to wonder if the risk was worth it. The main reason she had agreed to the terms was due to Amelia's designs. Without even realising it at the time, she was going to use them for Styles' new collection. Not only were they great designs but Amelia's idea about them being eco-friendly appealed to her conscience. This would also hook a lot of people in who were trying to do their small part for the planet.

'To you,' Vogue said, raising her glass in the air.

Melissa's eyes widened in surprise. 'Me? I didn't do anything.'

'Yes you did,' Vogue said, briefly touching Melissa's arm. 'You've stuck by me at a time others have walked away. I know I don't say it, and I know I can be hard work sometimes, but your loyalty means a lot to me.'

Melissa shrugged nonchalantly. 'It works both ways, I'm happy to be here.'

Vogue took a sip of wine as she continued to study Melissa. There was something about her demeanour that didn't sit right with her lately. She'd noticed Melissa's nervousness anytime they were alone. It was as if she wanted to say something but just couldn't muster the strength to do so. The reason Vogue hadn't pushed the issue was because deep down, she didn't want to know. She sensed it wouldn't be positive news. That Melissa was planning on jumping ship before it sank. Not that Vogue blamed her. These were uncertain times. Stressful times. When Melissa had joined the company, business had been thriving. Styles was 'the' company to work for.

But now that they were down to a skeleton work force, the buzz in the office wasn't the same as it once was. Hopefully, those days would soon be over.

Melissa traced her finger around the rim of her glass. 'I wish you would've told me you were going to take a loan out on your house.'

'Why?' Vogue asked, slightly confused how it would make a difference to Melissa what she did with her property.

'I dunno. I mean, do you really think this is all worth going bankrupt for?'

Vogue didn't answer straight away, unnerved by Melissa's direct question. A question that spoke volumes about her real thoughts on the situation.

'Are you saying you don't have faith in the collection being a success?'

'Let's just be realistic, the fashion industry isn't what it once was. People would rather buy clothes from Primark for a tenner than spend two hundred quid on a jacket just because it's got a Styles label on it.'

Vogue's heart sank as she realised there was truth in Melissa's words. 'Well, there goes my good mood.'

'Do you want me to lie to you, Vogue? Tell you everything's going to be all right? That one of your protégées are going to swoop in and save the day? Well, they're not.' Melissa paused, as if deciding whether to deliver the killer blow. 'I just don't think our brand has what it takes to survive in this current market. I'm sorry.'

'Then it's a good thing I've got more faith in Styles than you, isn't it?'

Vogue stood, downing the rest of her drink as she did so. She couldn't believe what she was hearing. Melissa was talking as if her company was a new kid on the block, not one with a proven history of designing clothes that people wanted to wear. Clothes that they were willing to pay over the odds for because they knew they were buying good quality garments that would last for years. Not the tat that was ruined after one wash.

'Come on, Vogue, I'm not saying these things to hurt you.'

'I know you're not but that doesn't make it hurt any less. I'll see you back at the office.'

With that, Vogue made her way to the exit. The last thing she needed in her life right now were disbelievers. Did Melissa really think Vogue was that naïve that she didn't know the size of the mountain she had to climb? Vogue knew more than anyone how difficult the road ahead was. The only difference was that she believed in her dream – the one that had been born many years ago, and she wasn't going to let go of it for anyone.

Especially for someone who was scared of their own shadow.

Chapter Twenty

Amelia kept her hands on her lap under the table. She didn't want Vogue to see them tremble. To know that she was vulnerable in her presence. That she had an effect on her like no one ever had.

It was strange, sitting in her office alone with her. If Vogue was feeling the same, she didn't show it. In fact, looking into her mesmerising eyes, all Amelia saw was a sense of calmness, nothing like the eruption taking place inside.

Seeing all of the awards framed on the wall and the expensive custom-made leather furniture, made her feel on edge and out of place. To say Amelia felt slightly intimidated was an understatement. By Vogue's obvious wealth, her confidence and her natural beauty. Every feature on her heart-shaped face was in perfect proportion, from her cute nose which curved ever so slightly at the tip, down to the deep dimples on her cheeks when she smiled. And what a killer smile she had.

Not once had she ever seen Vogue have a bad hair day. Her blonde sleek hair always seemed too perfect. Even after she'd had a few drinks.

As she sat waiting for Vogue to finish a phone call, Amelia wondered if it was the sexual attraction she felt towards her that was blowing her feelings for Vogue out of proportion. Under normal circumstances, by now she would have at least tried to make a move and let her feelings be known, verbally or physically. But fear stopped her from doing either.

'You look deep in thought.'

Amelia hadn't realised Vogue had finished on the phone.

'Do I?'

Vogue nodded. 'I take it you're wondering what I wanted to see you about?'

'I assume it's about my work?'

Vogue smiled. 'That and to tell you we're going to use your designs for our new outwear collection.'

Amelia couldn't believe what she was hearing. She didn't know whether to leap up off her chair and jump in the air screaming, or run around the desk and plant a whopping big kiss on Vogue's sensual mouth. As neither response was appropriate, Amelia tempered down her excitement and asked, 'Are you serious?'

'Yes.' There was a slight slur to Vogue's words and a faint whiff of alcohol which made Amelia question her decision-making abilities at that moment in time.

'But… do you really think my designs are good enough?' Amelia said, voicing her fear out loud. The worst thing that could happen was for her to get a call from Vogue the next day, telling her she'd made a mistake. A drunken mistake.

How many times had Amelia heard that one in her dating life? Too many to recall, especially in her early twenties.

When Vogue replied, the words were said with such sincerity that Amelia felt stupid for doubting her.

'Your work's as good as anyone else's I've seen. In fact, I'd go as far to say even better. You've got a unique talent, Amelia.'

The sound of her name on Vogue's lips made Amelia's insides melt. What she wouldn't have given to be able to kiss her right there and then. Just the thought of pressing her lips against Vogue's, caused a frisson of excitement to explode throughout her body.

This was not a normal reaction to have about someone that was totally out of her league.

Fuck!!! Come on, get yourself together. I'm not her type. And this is exactly what I need to stop doing. Fantasising.

She couldn't do this. Couldn't keep up this pretence.

If Amelia was going to have any success in keeping her emotions under wrap, her self-control had to improve. Otherwise she was going to go insane. Each thought about Vogue brought on a highly arousing, pleasant sensation. How the hell was Amelia going to get her out of her head? She knew Vogue spent way too much time in it, and it was detrimental, not only to her mental health, but the way she interacted with Vogue. How was Amelia supposed to do her job if she couldn't even look her boss in the eyes without wanting to do unthinkable things to her, *with her*? She couldn't and that was the problem. Unless Amelia wanted Vogue to start thinking she had social anxiety, she needed to snap out of this and grow up. It was a simple crush, no more, no less but she was letting it affect her in a way it shouldn't. It had to stop. For her own sake.

'Thanks.' Amelia forced herself to look straight at Vogue. Well, the space in-between her eyebrow area. To look directly into Vogue's eyes would have been emotional suicide.

'You don't think you're worth it, do you? You think I should use someone else's designs. That's why you don't seem overly pleased with the opportunity you've been given.'

Amelia's body tensed. How the hell had Vogue managed to detect her imposter syndrome? Her mind raced as it tried to come up with a way to rebuff her assertion, but she failed miserably.

'No, not at all. I mean, it's good to know you've got such faith in me…' Amelia's words trailed off. She was busted. Vogue could see straight through her and if she lied, all it would do is instil a level of distrust in her. Concluding she had nothing to lose, Amelia took a deep breath and readied herself to tell Vogue something she had never said out loud before – to anyone. Once it was out in the open, there was no taking it back.

'Yeah, you're right. I guess I still feel like a little kid inside with an adult exterior. I've never really felt my work was good enough. Even at university, there was always someone else who got singled out for their outstanding achievements.'

Vogue held her gaze. There were a million and one things Amelia could read into the way Vogue was staring back at her, but she was probably wrong on all counts. Amelia had tried to be open with Vogue, vulnerable to say the least, but Vogue hadn't responded. The least she could have done was say a few words of encouragement.

Feeling the size of an ant, Amelia jumped up suddenly. 'I need to use the ladies'.'

She could feel Vogue's gaze on her back as she hurried out of the room. Once in the corridor, Amelia made her way to the ladies' toilets. *Well done, Amelia. You've engaged your mouth before your brain can tell you to shut the fuck up.* And this was why she normally kept her thoughts and feelings to herself. No one could really understand the anxiety and turmoil that was hidden behind her smile. They just assumed because she was a healthy-looking woman, that was all there was to her. That she couldn't possibly be suffering in silence.

Little did they know.

And now Vogue had seen a glimpse into her mind, she was probably wondering why she had hired her, and even worse, why she was going to let Amelia design her new collection. Amelia could just imagine Vogue in her office now, trying to figure out how to backtrack on her offer.

One of these days I'll learn, Amelia told herself, knowing full well she wouldn't.

Amelia didn't know if she had the strength to go back out there and remain civil. The situation she found herself in was crazy. Cecile had warned her about Vogue, but she hadn't thought the woman would be able to get into her head and heart this quickly, or at all.

Amelia was still reeling from the suddenness of it all. The fireworks that exploded under her skin anytime she was near Vogue. The need and want to be close to her. To touch her. The playful sensuality in her eyes that felt like she was mentally undressing her.

Just this morning while she was sat at the kitchen table drinking her coffee, Amelia had imagined what it would be like to be sat across from Vogue, talking about their plans for that day. She knew it was crazy. That she had to get a grip if she wanted to keep working at Styles, but it wasn't as easy as turning it off like a switch. If it was, she would have done it from the time her feelings had started to overwhelm her.

The worst thing was that she didn't even have anyone to talk to about it. Cecile was normally her sounding board. The one she always turned to in her hour of need, but Amelia couldn't even do that now. She daren't tell any of her friends. They'd had just about enough of her dating stories.

Dating! That's it! What better way to take my mind off her than to go out on a date. Meet someone new.

But that didn't solve the immediate problem of finishing her meeting with Vogue, who by now must have been wondering what was taking her so long.

She was going to have to come up with an excuse to cut their meeting short, and she needed to do it sharpish. Her heart pounded faster and faster as she made her way back to Vogue's office. A quick intake of breath told her she couldn't sit back down. She just couldn't do it. Her legs felt like jelly as she walked in and held onto the table to support herself.

Before Amelia could come out with the first excuse, Vogue was out of her seat and beside her.

'You look a bit pale. Are you okay?' Vogue said, slipping her arm around Amelia's waist.

Why would you do that? a voice screamed in Amelia's head in response to Vogue's touch.

'Hey, you're trembling.'

You're touching me! How could I not tremble? 'I feel a bit sick, if I'm honest.'

'You should've told me,' Vogue said, her voice filled with concern.

'It's okay. I think I just need a bit of fresh air.'

'Come on then, let's go outside.'

'Don't worry, I'll be fine by myself. You get back to work.'

Vogue looked warily at her. 'Okay but I want you to go home if you don't feel any better.'

Amelia let out a sigh of relief when Vogue released her.

A few minutes after leaving Vogue's office, Amelia's fluttering pulse gradually resumed to a normal speed, but her world still felt off its axis.

How the hell am I going to work with her if she keeps making me feel like this?

Maybe it won't be so bad, Amelia told herself as she sat down at her desk and tried to focus on the design she'd been sketching.

I can't believe this is happening to me.

She buried her hands in her face in sheer frustration. When she looked up, the last person she expected to see was standing there. Nausea rose in her stomach for real this time. So much so that she nearly puked.

The shadow of disappointment on Cecile's face said it all.

'You've fallen for Vogue, haven't you?'

There was nowhere to run. Nowhere to hide. All Amelia could do was nod then bury her face in her hands again – this time in shame.

Chapter Twenty-One

Melissa arrived back at the office but decided against going to see if Vogue wanted her to run any errands. She knew she was the last person Vogue wanted to see as Melissa had burst her bubble by telling her the truth. *My version of the truth anyway*. The real truth was that Amelia was Styles' lifesaver. If Tina did take on the collection, there was a very good chance of Vogue regaining her solvency. Her house would also no longer be at risk.

If Vogue managed to turn her adversity into a success, all of Melissa's time and effort to destroy Vogue would have been wasted.

After wandering around in the lobby for a few minutes, pretending to be busy on her phone while she tried to figure out what to do with herself, she decided there was no point going home. All she'd do is drink wine and veg out in front of the TV with a takeaway. She could be doing something much more productive with her time.

Stuffing her phone into her pocket, Melissa walked decisively in the direction of the lift. Getting out on the second floor, she slowed her pace down as she reached the open-plan office. Though there were several people working at their desk or milling around near the photocopier, the atmosphere was sombre. Barely anyone spoke to each other or seemed to even acknowledge one another as they passed. It was a far cry from when Melissa had first started working there. Back then, Melissa was amazed to see staff members actually happy to arrive at work in the morning.

The office had a feel-good factor that she hadn't seen anywhere before. There was a closeness between them all. They were almost like family. Admittedly, she had felt a pang of jealousy at the way they would all sit around the conference room and finish each other's sentences as they spent hours brainstorming new ideas, long after they should have left for the day. It was almost as if Styles was their home.

But not anymore. Melissa had seen to that. It was right that Vogue's employees should be wondering what was going to happen, because the next event was going to cost them their jobs.

Looking around, Melissa saw Amelia at her desk, so totally engrossed in her work that she didn't seem to notice as Melissa stood behind her, looking over her shoulder. After remaining silent for a few moments, Melissa moved to her side and perched on the edge of Amelia's desk.

'Looking good.'

It took a few seconds for Amelia to glance up at her, and when she did, Melissa saw the glazed look in her eyes. The kind of look one got when nothing else in the world existed but the job at hand. She envied Amelia's ability to lose herself in something she obviously loved doing. Not that Melissa hadn't tried to at least develop one hobby, so she wasn't always alone. Working in a homeless shelter meant she was surrounded by those less fortunate than her and she tried her best to meet their needs. But after years of neglect, she found it difficult to connect with vulnerable people who needed someone to be empathetic to their cause. Not that she wasn't, she was whole-heartedly, but she couldn't express her emotions, couldn't reach them the way the other volunteers did, so in the end she gave up her spot for someone more suitable. Instead, she anonymously donated a large chunk of her wages at the end of each month. That way she was still of some use to the charity.

'Your sketch I mean,' Melissa said.

Amelia gave her a smile that didn't quite reach her eyes. There was something about her that reminded Melissa of herself. Not fully broken but not whole either. She easily recognised the signs in other people who didn't feel like they fit in. She knew the feeling all too well.

'Oh right, yeah it's okay.'

'If I had your ideas and talent, I'd be a millionaire by now.'

'It's not that good,' Amelia said with a wave of her hand.

'You're too modest.' Now that Amelia seemed more relaxed and open, it was time to test the waters. If Melissa wanted to move things forward, she was going to have to take some risks. 'So… I was wondering if you wanted to go out for a drink?'

'With you?'

'Yes, with me.'

Melissa saw a cloud of doubt cross Amelia's features. Had she got the timing wrong? Maybe it would have been better to suggest going out with Cecile too, so it was less full on.

Just as Melissa was about to suggest Cecile joining them, Amelia said, 'Sure, why not?'

'Really?' Melissa replied, taken aback by Amelia's answer. She had seriously thought she'd blown it. 'I mean, that's great.'

'Shall I meet you at BH1 after work?'

'Yeah.' Melissa got to her feet, not wanting to outstay her welcome. 'See you then.'

Melissa couldn't wipe the grin off her face. *Calm down idiot. She's only agreed to go for a drink, nothing more. I'm sure if it had been Vogue asking her out, she would've been a lot more enthusiastic.*

Melissa wasn't going to be too bothered about that. It was just a bump in the road. One that she would easily overcome once Styles had closed down. From then on, she'd never have to face competition with Vogue ever again. Especially when it came to Amelia.

And I'll finally get the girl.

Melissa left the office with a spring in her step at the thought of seeing Vogue's face on the day she finally got her just desserts.

***

Two empty bottles of wine and three empty packets of crisps littered the table. BH1 was packed, so they'd been lucky to get the two seats at the back of the bar. Because the place was so busy, it meant on more than one occasion Melissa had to lean in close in order to be heard.

Actual tears ran down Amelia's cheeks as she struggled to keep her composure.

'You're kidding me, she actually threatened to strut down the catwalk in her birthday suit 'cause she didn't have the outfit promised to her?'

'As God is my witness, it's true,' Melissa said, referring to yet another story of models behaving badly at fashion shows she'd attended in the past.

'That gets my vote for the most diva-like behaviour I've ever heard.'

Melissa raised her glass in agreement and Amelia mirrored her actions. It felt so good being in Amelia's company and having her full attention. If she was going to win at this game, she would have to play her cards right. She couldn't be too pushy. From what Melissa had sussed out about her so far, Amelia was very insecure about herself. Not in an immature way. More so because she hadn't found herself yet. She seemed to still be stuck in that in-between place where she relied on the outside world to define her, rather than just being herself. It was something Melissa had long suffered with, and it was only as she got older that she realised the outside world had no relevance to her true character. That's why she had no social media accounts. The days of needing validation from an outside source were well and truly gone.

'How're you finding working at Styles?' Melissa asked, looking for some common ground to have a more meaningful conversation. She wanted Amelia to trust her. To open up to her.

Melissa didn't miss the flicker in Amelia's eyes at the mention of Styles. It could only mean one thing, but she prayed it wasn't so.

Please don't tell me they've already slept together! Because if they had, her plan would fail for sure. If Amelia and Vogue had been intimate, there would be no way of putting a wedge between them.

Damn! Why didn't I intervene sooner?

'So far so good. Vogue seems happy with my work.' Amelia leant forward and whispered in a conspiratorial tone. 'Being her personal assistant, you probably already know, but I'm bursting to tell everyone that she's going to use my designs for her outwear collection. I haven't even told Cecile yet.'

Melissa's heart sank at the sight of Amelia's obvious happiness. It truly made her feel like the worst person in the world, knowing that she was going to be the one responsible for taking her happiness away from her.

Melissa played with the stem of her glass. She fought with herself as to whether her next sentence would make her look like a complete bitch in Amelia's eyes. In the end, her head overruled her heart. She had to follow through with her plan. She couldn't allow for emotions to derail it.

'I wouldn't be so fast to finish your designs, if I

was you.'

The smile on Amelia's face disappeared in an instant, replaced with a frown of confusion. 'What does that mean?'

'Meaning.' Melissa paused for dramatic effect. 'That you might get caught up in the crossfire when the shit hits the fan, and you know what they say about birds of a feather, you'll be tarred with the same brush. Vogue isn't the person you think she is. Trust me, I should know.'

'Oh.' Amelia's stare didn't waver, but Melissa could see she was crushed by the news.

'Look, I'm telling you this in confidence,' Melissa continued, leaning forward, hoping she hadn't misread Amelia as someone who kept her word. 'So this goes no further than the two of us, right?'

Amelia nodded in agreement.

Melissa took a sip of wine, drawing out the tension. 'Vogue was involved in a scandal a while back—'

'What kind of scandal?' Amelia asked with a puzzled expression.

'I can't tell you, not now, but she's not out of the woods yet—'

'But what's this got to do with my designs?'

Melissa tried to sound as sincere as possible. Amelia didn't strike her as someone who would take anyone's word at face value. She had to gain her trust. *Slowly, slowly catchy monkey.*

'Everything. Just trust me on this… delay finishing your designs. That way when it all blows up, you can walk away unscathed with your work. I have contacts in the industry who would be more than happy for you to join their team.'

'You're the second person that's warned me about Vogue. I genuinely thought she was a nice person.'

Melissa felt a huge sense of relief at her revelation being validated. She had been relying on the fact that Cecile would have bad-mouthed Vogue to Amelia at some stage. She didn't know exactly what had happened, but something had occurred between the two women to cause the discord she sensed whenever they were together. Melissa had never asked Vogue about it because their relationship wasn't the type where they shared details of their personal lives. Not that Melissa would have wanted Vogue as a shoulder to cry on.

With Cecile, though they were on friendly terms, Melissa had never encouraged her to open up as she didn't have the bandwidth to take on other people's problems. It was hard enough dealing with her own.

'See. The only reason I'm telling you is because… well… I like you.'

At this Amelia smiled. What she was conveying by this, Melissa didn't know, but she took it as a positive sign. Especially when Amelia got up and went to the bar.

Melissa watched as Amelia ordered another round of drinks.

Amelia glanced back, still smiling.

It looked like she was in with a chance after all.

Chapter Twenty-Two

There was one rule Vogue tried to live by, and that was to face the truth no matter how hard or painful it was. That was what she was going to do now – face up to the fact that she was on her own. It wasn't fair, but then life wasn't fair. It was what you made it.

Sitting in her office surrounded by awards of achievement, she was still surprised at how quickly her life had fallen down around her. The fact that she'd been able to conceal the accusations made against her was a feat in itself. The fashion industry was well known for its love of gossip, and taking any opportunity to step over another company if it meant them getting to the top. It was a testament to the loyalty of her staff, and that's why she couldn't afford to fail. Even if Melissa did think it was an impossibility.

The way Melissa had suddenly switched on her, made Vogue wonder if she'd been holding those sentiments about the company all this time. She had stupidly thought Melissa had believed in her, so it was a shock to realise she didn't. But Melissa's opinion wouldn't stop Vogue from rising to the top. If anything, she was going to use it as fuel to propel her even higher this time. Feeling the determination rise within, Vogue was going to bypass the stage she had been at – she was going to come back better. Stronger. Nothing or no one was going to get in her way.

It saddened her to think of the last meeting with

Amelia. Where she had opened up about her lack of self-belief. Vogue had been speechless at how little she thought of herself. So much so, Vogue couldn't find the words to explain to Amelia how amazingly talented and special she was. By the time she had found her voice, Amelia had made a quick exit.

A tap on the door caused Vogue to push thoughts of Amelia aside. She had already made the decision next time she saw her, to have a heart to heart. Hopefully, Vogue would be able to make Amelia see her self-worth.

'Come in,' Vogue said when she saw Trudy standing in the doorway.

Trudy walked in, her demeanour edgy and nervous.

'Trudy,' Vogue said smiling. 'How can I help?'

Vogue liked to have an open-door policy with her staff. That way they could tell when things were going wrong, as well as when they were going right.

'Um, I don't know how to say this.'

'Just saying it as it is normally helps,' Vogue said, gesturing for Trudy to take a seat which she did.

Vogue searched Trudy's face to pick up on any cues. The woman had only been working for her for a few weeks and, as far as she knew, everything had been running smoothly on the floor below.

'I… I think someone's stolen my designs.'

Vogue almost choked upon hearing Trudy's words. Whether it was caused by a trigger from the past in dealing with Bev, she didn't know, but she had to force herself to maintain her composure and keep in the present moment.

'Oh,' Vogue said, 'What makes you think that?'

'It's just that….' Trudy paused and looked bewildered for a moment. As if trying to work out whether her accusation was real, or whether she had somehow misplaced her designs somewhere.

'Go on,' Vogue pressed gently.

Either way, Trudy was in the hot seat now and her words had been spoken. She had no choice but to follow through.

'I left my designs in my desk drawer overnight. I normally take them home, but I was going out last night.'

Vogue kept her hands under her desk out of view. She didn't want Trudy to see her fingers twisting, a habit of hers when she wanted someone to get to the point rather than go around the houses with meaningless details.

'Right,' Vogue said, nodding her head in encouragement.

Trudy combed her fingers through her thin hair. 'I just checked and they're gone.'

Vogue inwardly shuddered. Did they have a thief working there or was it a simple misunderstanding? Maybe someone else moved it. Why they would randomly go into Trudy's drawer, Vogue didn't know, but it was a possibility. Her mum used to be constantly moving her stuff around when she lived at home.

'Leave this with me, Trudy. We'll get to the bottom of things. Have you got another copy of the designs?'

Trudy shook her head. 'My work's original. I never

make copies.'

'Well, maybe this is a sign that you should. Just as a precaution.' Vogue smiled again. The outer calm belied the apprehension inside. 'And I'd prefer to keep this between us until I find out what's happened.'

'Of course,' Trudy said, her expression still maintaining a look of helplessness.

Vogue glanced at her watch to give the impression she was short for time. Trudy took the hint and rose to her feet.

As soon as Trudy closed the door behind her, Vogue picked up her phone. It was an additional expense that she didn't need but she would not let this situation spiral out of control.

'Nick,' Vogue said when he answered the phone. 'I want four desks with locks on the drawers delivered today.'

'Today? But—'

'I don't want to hear any buts. I just want it done.' This wasn't said in a demanding, throwing her toys out of her pram, tone. It was said in a way to convey the urgency the situation required. There was no way on earth Vogue was going to travel down that same road again. She had done it once with Bev and that was more than enough.

'Okay.'

'Thanks, Nick.'

Vogue disconnected the call. She could only sense what lay ahead if anyone found out designs were going missing. That their workspace wasn't safe. Up until now, even after what Bev had put Vogue and her team through, there was still a sense of trust between them all. Another case of dishonesty could push them over the edge.

Vogue took the lift down to the floor below on the pretence of checking the office out.

What am I doing here?

It only took a glimpse of Amelia sat at her desk in deep concentration, for her to admit the truth to herself.

It still amazed her that Amelia had come into her life and turned it upside down. Especially at a time when she needed to have her full attention on getting her business back on its feet. The last thing she needed was a distraction, and such an attractive one at that. She liked it best when Amelia wore her hair in a ponytail, like she did today, as it showed off the perfect symmetry of her face

As if sensing Vogue was thinking about her, Amelia looked up.

Caught, with no way back, Vogue did the only thing she could – awkwardly waved at her.

Amelia waved back, smiling broadly.

Vogue turned around and walked back down the corridor, left to wonder what the hell she was going to do.

Chapter Twenty-Three

Amelia gazed at Vogue as she walked away, and her heart sank. What did she think she was doing waving so enthusiastically at her boss? Had she lost her senses? She must have looked like a grinning idiot. Amelia cringed.

Playing it cool has never been my strong point.

It was too late to do anything now. Her thoughts returned to Melissa. She'd advised Amelia to keep her distance but how could she? To do so would only make Vogue suspicious, especially if Amelia was to tell her she was having issues with her designs. While Amelia had no reason to doubt Melissa's intentions, she couldn't help but pit her gut feeling against Melissa's revelation that Vogue was not to be trusted.

At no time during any of their interactions did Amelia sense that Vogue was dishonest. In truth, she found her to be very open and upfront about things. But then there was Cecile's opinion to add to the mix. It was one thing doubting Melissa, as she didn't really know her that well, but she had known Cecile forever and she trusted her implicitly. As such, she had absolutely no reason to lie to her.

Why does everything have to be so bloody complicated?

All Amelia wanted to do was work at a job that she loved more than anything. All of these complications and dramas only served as a distraction.

'Hey, how's it going?' Jordan appeared out of nowhere with a wide smile on her face. This wouldn't have been so surprising if she'd made any attempt to talk to Amelia in the weeks that they'd been sat opposite one another, but she hadn't. Jordan had ignored any attempt Amelia made to befriend her, so she was a little perplexed as to why she was suddenly being so nice.

Amelia had genuinely thought Jordan disliked her. Not that it bothered her in the slightest. Not everyone was going to take to her. In the end, she had put it down to professional competition and left it at that.

'Yeah, things are good thanks,' Amelia said. 'You?'

'No complaints.' Jordan paused. 'Yet, anyway.'

'You say that like you're expecting trouble.'

'Not really. But I'm sure you know how these things work, once the pressure's on, things are going to get pretty heated. Dog eat dog, if you know what I mean?'

Amelia nodded in agreement despite feeling uncomfortable that Vogue still hadn't told anyone that she was going to use Amelia's designs. It made her feel dishonest to watch her colleagues hard at work on a project that wasn't going to come to fruition. Unless Vogue's plan was to use them for another collection.

That made sense when she thought about it. It wasn't as if Styles could afford to only have one collection.

'How're your designs coming along?'

Jordan tapped her nose. 'Now that would be telling, wouldn't it?'

'I was just wondering, that's all.'

'I'm not a sharer, unlike yourself it seems.'

'I haven't got anything to hide.' Amelia turned her drawing around for Jordan to see. She was confident that her own style was unique and wasn't worried about anyone trying to steal her ideas.

'Pretty impressive,' Jordan said, taking the drawing in with widened eyes. 'Oh, what the hell, can I make a small suggestion?'

'Of course.'

'That collar would look better like this.' Jordan picked up a pencil and added a small adjustment to the drawing.

Amelia turned the paper back around to face her and almost gasped. 'You're so right. Oh my God, I didn't even think of that. Thank you.'

'You're welcome, but don't expect too many favours, we're competitors,' Jordan said with a wink.

Though Jordan was trying to make light of her comment, Amelia knew she was deadly serious, but she didn't care. The fact that Jordan had helped improve her design when she could have simply said nothing, spoke volumes about the woman's generous nature.

'I owe you a drink.'

'Did I hear someone mention a drink?'

Amelia looked past Jordan just as Melissa came into view. At first, she was happy to see her, but then had a sudden thought. Melissa was Vogue's personal assistant. What if when this so-called bombshell landed, Melissa was part of it too. Amelia's temples pounded and she felt herself wishing she was back in Bournemouth where her life had been so simple. She knew where she stood with the people around her, unlike at Styles. Suddenly, she didn't know who she could trust and that actually scared her. This kind of environment was not what she had expected when happily taking on the job.

'Yeah,' Amelia said. 'I was just asking Jordan to join me for one so we can discuss our work.'

'Oh,' Melissa said with a look of disappointment. Melissa remained standing there, as if waiting for her invite. When it wasn't forthcoming, the penny seemed to drop. 'Good idea. Glad to see two women getting along without letting the competitive edge come between you.'

If it was one thing Amelia couldn't understand, it was the scarcity mentality that some people seemed to have. The way Amelia's mind worked, she was happy to lend support to whoever needed it. Competitor or not.

'Maybe we can hang out another time?' Melissa said to Amelia.

Jordan looked at them both with an enquiring gaze.

'Yeah, sure,' Amelia said. She knew she was doing the right thing being non-committal until figuring out who she could trust.

So why didn't it feel that way?

Chapter Twenty-Four

'This is not my problem, Vogue.' Melissa stood by the window in her office, her back to Vogue who, when she'd walked in minutes earlier, looked like she was on the verge of a meltdown. This gave Melissa a high she'd never experienced before. For the first time in their relationship, the scales had tipped in Melissa's favour. Now she was the one with the upper hand.

'Not your problem?' Vogue looked at her incredulously. 'Do you know how hard it is to ask for your help?'

Melissa was well aware of the difficulty Vogue had in showing any weakness. She was rattled – badly. It was like the Bev incident all over again. Only this time Vogue had a lot more to lose, as she no longer had enough money to keep going.

'That's where you're wrong. You aren't asking for help to improve a situation. You're asking me to help you drag up the past. Something that should be left exactly where it is. Buried and forgotten.'

Melissa turned to face Vogue, hands on hips, her stomach filled with butterflies in anticipation. She had to play her part in this right. If she gave the slightest hint that she knew the reason behind Vogue's plea for help, it would cause suspicion and that was the last thing she needed if her plan was to succeed.

'What's caused this sudden change of heart? I thought you never wanted to hear her name ever mentioned again?'

'I know, but I need closure.' Vogue's tone was absolute as she raised her fingers to her temple.

'But why now, after all this time?'

'So I can finally move on.'

How many times had Melissa heard herself saying those exact words to her therapist? *Too many to count.*

'I'll ask again, why now?' Melissa pressed. 'You could've had closure when this all happened.' *But you decided to run and hide instead of facing it head on.*

Melissa savoured the moment, seeing the uncertainty in Vogue's eyes. The fear of being faced with something she had zero control over. It exhilarated Melissa to know that such a small act on her behalf, could have made such a big impact. In fact, if Vogue wasn't standing right there in front of her, Melissa would have given herself a congratulatory pat on the back. After all, she had managed to execute her plan to trigger Vogue, down to perfection.

The only thing that had taken her by surprise was Vogue wanting to make contact with Bev again. That had completely blindsided her. Not that it was going to be a problem, far from it. She was actually looking forward to catching up with Bev again, if only to find out the catalyst for her sudden return.

'Trudy's designs were taken from her drawer,' Vogue said as if the words were being forced out of her mouth.

'Taken? By who?' Melissa feigned shock. If her drama teacher could see her now, she'd be proud of her.

Even Melissa was impressed by her believable performance.

'That's just it, I don't know. I think Bev has someone on the inside here working for her.'

Melissa let out a quick laugh. 'No disrespect intended, but you can't seriously believe that. I mean, for what reason?'

'I don't know, it seems like she just wants to ruin me. That's why I want you to go and see her. Let her know I'm onto her little scheme and she's not going to get away with it, not this time.'

'I'm sorry to have to say this,' Melissa said, trying to convey a sympathy she didn't feel in the slightest. 'But I think the stress of this situation is clouding your judgement.'

As soon as the words left her mouth, Melissa knew she'd crossed the line. Vogue's eyes narrowed as they bored into her own.

'You think I'm imagining all this? Isn't that what you said when I first became suspicious about Bev?'

Melissa put her hands in the air as a sign of submission. 'Yes and I apologised for that mistake, but this is a different situation altogether. What exactly would she do with Trudy's designs?'

'It's not about the designs, Melissa. It's about trying to destroy my reputation again.'

Melissa conceded that she had put up enough resistance to make Vogue think she was opposed to her idea but would go along with it to keep the peace.

'Okay, fine, I'll go and have a chat with Bev. See

what I can find out.'

'Thanks.' Vogue took a step forward, placing her hand on Melissa's shoulder.

'No need to thank me. You know you can always count on me.'

You can also count on me to be right by your side when your empire comes crashing down and I walk off with the prize.

Amelia.

Chapter Twenty-Five

You're your own worst enemy, Vogue told herself as she took a seat at BH1's bar. *Always on the lookout for trouble where none exists.* Why had she mentioned her concerns to Melissa? Melissa had made her thoughts on the subject quite clear. That Vogue was buckling under the stress of things. Maybe she was, but Vogue just couldn't rid herself of that niggling feeling in her gut that something wasn't right, which was why she had taken the unprecedented step of involving Melissa in her plan.

At no point was she expecting Bev to make a full confession, even if she was up to no good. All she hoped to achieve was to fire a warning signal in Bev's direction to let her know she was aware of what she was trying to do. The business was at a crucial stage and she couldn't afford for any gossip to come out about Styles. It would be suicidal for both Vogue and the business. And as much as Melissa protested against her reasoning as to why she thought the theft had something to do with Bev, nothing could persuade Vogue that she wasn't behind it in some way. The truth was, there was a real possibility that Bev could have someone doing her dirty work for her. After all, she had been working at Styles for years and had her loyal followers who stayed on after Vogue had given Bev the boot. Vogue wasn't that naïve to not think people still held a grudge against her for letting Bev go, despite what she'd done.

It amazed her that their group of mutual friends

had thought Vogue should have rolled over and tried to move on with Bev still onside. The very idea was inconceivable. Trust was the one value that she held above all others. Once that was gone, there was nothing left.

'What'll it be?'

The barwoman was someone she hadn't seen before. Though Vogue wasn't in the best of moods, she gave her a quick smile as she ordered her drink. Minutes later, the barwoman placed a large gin and tonic in front of her.

Vogue was going to do her best to keep her drinking down to a minimum. The last thing she wanted or needed was a hangover. The older she got, the less it seemed to take to put her in the dreaded 'depressive mode', where she walked around feeling like death for days. Like everything else, age just seemed to catch up with her without her even realising it.

Vogue checked her phone. *Nothing.* Melissa said she'd update her once she'd made contact with Bev. The fact that she hadn't so much as messaged her, could only mean two things. Either Bev couldn't be found, or she had refused to talk to Melissa.

Maybe the latter would be for the best, she reasoned. It wasn't as if Vogue had made the decision in a rational state of mind. Far from it. She'd been in a panic. If word got out a theft had taken place in her company, no matter how small, she could kiss goodbye to any chance of getting her collection into Milan.

'Hi.'

Vogue recognised the voice but couldn't place it. She turned her head sideways and came face to face with Jordan.

'Hey, how's it going?' Vogue said, feeling slightly awkward at meeting Jordan inside a bar at five p.m.

Though Jordan been working at Styles a few weeks now, Vogue hadn't really had much to do with her. This wasn't by design, as Vogue enjoyed interacting with her colleagues, it was simply down to the fact that she had higher priorities.

'Good, thanks. Can I get you another one?' Jordan said, looking down at Vogue's empty glass.

'Oh, um sure,' Vogue said, not even aware how much she'd drank already.

Vogue couldn't think of a single word to say to Jordan, and it seemed to be a mutual feeling as they both remained silent while the barwoman poured their drinks. Not that she was being anti-social, she just had a lot on her mind.

Vogue willed her phone to ring so she could find out if Melissa had managed to speak to Bev.

'Why don't you come and join us,' Jordan said as she turned to leave.

'I'm fine,' Vogue replied, raising her glass. 'But thanks for the drink.'

'Well, if you change your mind, we're over there,' Jordan said, nodding her head towards a space in the corner of the bar.

Fuck! Vogue nearly said the word out loud, such was the shock of seeing Amelia sat looking down at her phone. Vogue doubted Amelia had seen her. What should she do? Make a quick escape? How stupid would that look? A grown woman running away like a frightened child. The only alternative was to stop overthinking and just get on with finishing her drink. Then go home.

'I'm going after this,' Vogue finally said.

'Well, enjoy,' Jordan said before walking off to join Amelia.

Vogue stole a glance in their direction as Jordan reached their table and Amelia looked over at her in response to something Jordan had said.

The rollercoaster of Vogue's emotions was driving her insane. She needed to sort her head out before she totally lost it.

Vogue turned her attention back to her drink in an attempt to block Amelia out. This was short-lived, as moments later someone brushed up against her. It didn't take a genius to figure out who it was.

'Guess you didn't see me wave hello,' Amelia said, the sarcasm obvious in her voice.

Vogue looked up at her, her body reacting way before her mind did. Tingling sensations ran from head to foot. Heart palpitations thumped in her chest. Her hands trembled, causing the liquid in the glass she held to sway gently from side to side.

Vogue immediately put the glass down on the bar and pressed her hands on her thighs to regain some semblance of control.

'Guess I didn't,' Vogue replied as coolly as she could.

Neither spoke for a few moments, then Amelia said, with a teasing flicker in her eyes, 'You always drink alone?'

Vogue's stomach constricted with what felt like hundreds of butterflies darting around in mayhem. 'You always so inquisitive?'

'Yeah, bad habit from childhood.'

'Bet your mum was pleased.'

'She was actually,' Amelia said, her eyes sparkling with amusement.

'Good for her.'

Amelia observed her in silence, her eyes roaming down to her mouth then back again up to her eyes.

'So, you planning on driving home again tonight?' Amelia's voice was low, like they were having an intimate moment.

Vogue looked straight at her, the feeling of attraction startling her. 'Why? You offering to take me instead?'

Vogue almost laughed out loud at Amelia's expression. For a woman that exuded so much self-control, it was the first time she'd seen Amelia lose her composure. *Maybe she does feel something for me after all.*

'That would be a bit rude considering I came here with someone else.'

'Oh well,' Vogue said, getting to her feet.

Standing barely inches apart, the intensity of their chemistry hung in the thickness of the air. Their eyes locked on one another's and Vogue was achingly aware that it would take less than a second for her to shift forward and press her mouth against Amelia's. To part her lips with the tip of her tongue and enter her warm, wet mouth. Vogue glanced at Amelia's exposed cleavage revealed by the undone buttons of her white shirt.

Just the thought of what she would like to do to Amelia there and then, had Vogue spinning away in the opposite direction in an attempt to break the connection. She was not used to this sort of cat and mouse game. Any other woman, she would have already slept with her. But this was something new. Not that she didn't want to. She did very much. But she was enjoying the build-up. The push and pull dynamic. For some reason, it just made it all the more exciting for her.

'I'd better make a move,' Vogue said without giving Amelia a second glance.

If she did, Amelia would be able to see right through her, but Vogue wasn't ready to reveal all her cards.

Not yet anyway.

Chapter Twenty-Six

Vogue had walked out of the bar an hour earlier, yet every inch of Amelia's body was still on high alert. She didn't know how she felt about her anymore. While Amelia still thought she was an amazing woman because of what she'd achieved with Styles, she couldn't help but feel as if she'd been duped. That she was being played with. *Is this just a game to her?*

One minute she was warm and friendly and the next, cold and dismissive. After spotting her in the bar, it had taken all the confidence Amelia could muster, plus some Dutch courage, to approach her. It seemed like they were flirting, well in Amelia's head they were, but Vogue leaving abruptly without saying goodbye, just served to reinforce Amelia's insecurities.

Cecile's words played on her mind. *Vogue can't be trusted. She's like a chameleon. She'll break your heart.*

'Helllllooooo, anybody home?'

Jordan's sing song voice filtered into Amelia's mind, stopping her dead in her thoughts. 'Sorry, I was miles away.'

'Yeah, I noticed.'

'Were you asking me something?'

'Yes, I asked you what your plans were and if you would stay on at Styles after the probation period.'

Amelia frowned. She hadn't thought that far ahead, especially in light of what Melissa told her. If Jordan had asked her that same question a few days ago, it would have been an emphatic yes without a doubt. But now she wasn't so sure.

Could Amelia continue to work with someone she had unrequited feelings for, on top of the other issues? She wasn't so sure.

What if Melissa was right, and whatever the bombshell was, would tarnish everyone who worked at Styles? If it was bad enough to get the public's attention, Amelia could just imagine her next interview where she would have to state that she had worked there, regardless of how long it had been for. The very thought of what her name could become entangled with, made her wonder if she should jump ship now.

Amelia swallowed down the lump that suddenly formed in her throat at the thought of leaving Styles, and more importantly Vogue. 'I don't know…'

'But what would you do if you didn't?'

'Go back to my old life,' Amelia said. Although Melissa had been kind enough to offer to find her another job, Amelia didn't think she'd have the heart for it. Remaining in London would be too hard for her. Never knowing if she might bump into Vogue or hear some random gossip about her. At least if she went back to Bournemouth, she could limit the exposure of a life without Vogue in it.

'What's your old life then?' Jordan said, eyeing her intensely.

'Retail during the day. Working my arse off on my designs during the night.'

Jordan rose to her feet and moved to sit next to

Amelia. 'What if I suggested something different... I mean, assuming neither of us want to stay here.'

'Go on,' Amelia said, interested to hear about a possible plan B.

'We could go into business together,' Jordan said as if she'd just announced the blueprint for a never thought of before idea.

'Doing what?'

'Your new designs. I know someone who would be willing to manufacture them if he gets a decent cut. Then we can sell them on the internet.'

Amelia's heart dropped. She thought Jordan was going to come up with a solid plan, not one that Amelia herself had tried and failed at several times. To make noise in an already overcrowded marketplace was going to take more than talent to breakthrough. It needed money, and that was one thing Amelia didn't have. By the looks of it, Jordan didn't have much either.

Realising that heading back to Bournemouth was more than likely going to be a reality, her sadness at the thought of losing touch with Vogue tore at her heart again. It wasn't as if someone of Vogue's calibre would have much to do with her once she was out of sight anyway. She'd probably forget Amelia by the time she boarded her train.

'I thought you were ambitious?' The disappointment in Jordan's voice was evident.

'I am, but I'm also a realist. There are so many outgoings to running your own business, and the type of job I'd be able to get would just pay me enough to live, let alone run a business as well.'

'Okay, well it was just a thought.' Jordan sighed as she grabbed her jacket. 'Suppose we'd better get a move on. It's getting late.'

'I haven't upset you, have I?' Amelia asked in response to Jordan's sudden mood change.

'No, don't be silly. I'll ask one of the other girls at work. They'll probably have better designs anyway.'

With that, Jordan slipped into her jacket and without another word, left the bar.

Amelia stared at the exit as the door closed, trying to make sense of what had just taken place between them. *What the fuck was that about? Am I going mad?*

Amelia couldn't believe Jordan would react in such a childish manner.

And insulting me as well. Is anybody normal in this world?

Feeling slightly put out, Amelia was grateful Cecile was at home when she got back to her flat. After relaying their conversation, Cecile was as outraged at Jordan's behaviour as she was, which softened the blow a little.

'I told you,' Cecile said, painting the last toenail on her foot bright pink. 'There're a lot of weirdos out there, especially—'

'All right, you don't have to say her name,' Amelia said, knowing full well Cecile was talking about Vogue. Since Amelia's confession to her having a crush on Vogue, Cecile had made her promise she wouldn't act on it, no matter what.

At the time, Amelia had agreed, but had her fingers

crossed. It was a childish gesture, but she didn't want to tempt fate and get a run of bad luck if she crossed the line.

'Have you seen her?' Cecile said, making it clear she was talking about Vogue.

Amelia nodded.

'And?' Cecile placed the nail polish brush back in the bottle and eyed her suspiciously as she tightened the lid.

'And nothing,' Amelia said, keeping her gaze glued to her phone. If Cecile caught sight of her expression, she'd be able to read her mind. In between being annoyed with herself for letting Jordan's standoffish behaviour get to her, her thoughts lingered on the intense few minutes she'd spent with Vogue at the bar. Amelia replayed the events again in her head. Vogue's wet lips as she took a sip of her drink, her dark arched eyebrows raising at Amelia's response to her question about driving her home, the cold detached way she got up and left.

Wait, did she want me to go home with her?

The realisation suddenly hit Amelia and she put her head in her hands.

I've completely misread the situation. She must think I'm the one playing games!

'What's wrong?' Cecile's voice broke into her reverie.

'Oh, erm, nothing. No, she was just leaving as I arrived.'

Amelia couldn't tell Cecile how right the attraction

between them felt when Cecile would only tell her how wrong it was.

Amelia also wasn't about to tell her why she was going to have an early night, and what she was going to do to herself once she was alone with her thoughts of Vogue.

Only she was privy to that.

And if the bombshell Melissa had referred to ended up being nothing more than a blip, she hoped her feelings for Vogue wouldn't be.

Chapter Twenty-Seven

The wooden front door slowly opened, Bev's apprehensive features just about visible in the open crack.

'I wondered how long it would be before you showed your face.' The distaste at seeing Melissa was evident in her voice.

'Nice to see you too, Bev,' Melissa said, quickly jamming her foot between the door and frame to prevent Bev from shutting her out. With one forceful movement, Melissa pushed on the door, causing Bev to nearly lose her balance as she took a step backwards, glaring at Melissa as she brushed past her and made her way into the living room.

Looking around the room, Melissa wasn't surprised to see the numerous framed photos of Bev and her husband that had once adorned the walls were now gone. As sad as it was, some people just weren't meant to be together.

'What do you want?' Bev, a statuesque, elegant woman, entered the room tentatively. Her eyes trained on Melissa as if preparing herself for an imminent attack.

Melissa laughed at Bev's behaviour. She had never been violent towards anyone in her life and had no intention of starting now. 'That's not very hospitable now, is it? It's been what? Eight months?'

'Just say your piece, Melissa, and get out of my sight. Just looking at you makes me feel sick.'

'That's not what you said the last time I saw you.'

Bev's expression turned from disgust into a scowl. 'Things are different now. You've got nothing to hold over me anymore.'

'No, I suppose you're right, but that doesn't stop me from wondering why you came back after all this time.'

Bev's eyes narrowed into slits. Melissa half expected her to growl and pounce on her. 'This is my home.'

'Yes but we had an agreement. Remember?'

Bev snorted. 'How could I forget? You took everything from me—'

'No, Bev,' Melissa said, taking a seat and making herself comfortable. 'Your downfall was your own doing, remember that, if—'

'Does Vogue know what a prized cunt you are yet? Or are you still being covert, pretending to be a loyal lap dog?'

Melissa laughed at this. Bev made her sound so… Machiavellian. 'Yeah, it's the same ole, same ole. Vogue's still as trusting as ever.'

'You're one sick bitch, you know that?'

'So you said.' Melissa rose to her feet. 'Look, I don't want to be here anymore than you want me to be, so I'll get straight to the point.'

Melissa walked over to Bev, stopping barely an inch away from her.

Bev took a step back. Melissa took a step forward, closing the gap again. Her intention to merely intimidate.

'If you've come back to tell Vogue the truth, you'd

better get that bright idea right out of your head.'

Bev took a step back. 'I don't need to tell her. She'll suss you out eventually.'

'Yeah, she might but it'll be too late then. She won't have a business left to run and her name won't be worth shit.'

'You tried before and it didn't work,' Bev reminded her.

'Maybe not. But this time around, I'm a lot wiser. Smarter. And I know exactly what I need to do.'

'Why do you hate her so much?' Bev asked, shaking her head slowly as her eyes welled with tears. 'What's she ever done to you but be kind?'

'Kind? Kind?' Melissa's voice rose to such a level, Bev winced in fear. 'Do you even know the meaning of the word?'

Forcing herself to inhale a deep breath, Melissa said, 'Keep away from Vogue. If I so much as see you within a foot of her....'

Melissa fixed Bev with a stare that she hoped would send her a message loud and clear. *Don't even think about fucking me over.*

Only two women had done that to her in her life, one was Vogue and the other had been her own mother. Her *mother* who had given Melissa up for adoption when she was one but had soon gone on to have another baby.

Vogue.

Only, she decided to keep that baby.

***

Seeing four missed calls and two text messages from Vogue, Melissa resisted the urge to block her to avoid seeing her name altogether. *One day.*

Melissa moved on to the message underneath. Now this was the one she'd been waiting for. Opening it, her eyes quickly scanned the message and what she read was not what she wanted at all. Quite the opposite in fact. Amelia had not taken Jordan's bait.

At least Amelia has loyalty, even if it is with the wrong person.

Melissa tapped the steering wheel with her finger, lost in thought. Should she tell Jordan to back off, now she knew Amelia wouldn't part ways with Styles? Yet, anyway.

Getting Vogue to hire Melissa's old school friend, Jordan, as one of the trainees, had been easier than she'd expected. Especially as Jordan didn't know the difference between a button and a zip.

It had only cost Melissa a few hundred pounds to have a freelancer knock up some original designs. Jordan didn't have to be asked twice. Once Melissa explained her plan, she was more than happy to help.

But now what did she do? There were two weeks left before the designs for the collection had to be ready. Two weeks of thinking up ideas that would cause mayhem at Styles, or was it time to bring everything to a head?

Starting the engine, Melissa drove off, her mind still racing. She couldn't really use Bev again, or could she? To use her presence to unbalance Vogue before she went in for the kill? To give the impression Bev was back to do even more harm?

Pulling over to the side of the road, she quickly dialled Vogue's number and waited for her to answer.

'I've been trying to reach you for ages,' Vogue said, the desperation for answers evident in her voice.

'Sorry, I just left her place.'

'And? What did she say?'

'She didn't admit to any wrongdoing, neither did she deny it.'

'What the fuck does that mean?'

'It means exactly what I said. She wouldn't open up to me. But I can tell she's got something up her sleeve. She kind of had this self-satisfied smirk on her face.'

Melissa could just imagine Vogue pacing the floor as her words sunk in.

'I knew it. I fucking knew it.'

'I've got a bad feeling about this, Vogue.'

'Me too.' Vogue let out a soft sigh. 'Thanks for going to see her for me. I really appreciate it.'

'Hey, I told you I'll do anything to help. I'll be by your side until the end.'

'Just knowing that makes me feel a lot better.'

'Good. I'm heading home now. See you tomorrow.'

'Yeah, see you tomorrow. Get a good night's sleep.'

'You too.'

A few minutes later, Melissa logged into the

Twitter profile she had set up when she was originally going to break the story of Vogue's and Bev's plagiarism. After Vogue's payoff she'd decided to bide her time.

'Styles' plagiarism costs Vogue one million! Now idea of trainee designer is stolen.'

Melissa smiled as she pressed 'tweet'.

You're damn right I'm going to get a good night's sleep.

Chapter Twenty-Eight

Vogue sat on the wooden bench beside her mother's grave, her watery gaze fixed on the date inscription on the granite headstone. 1965-2020. Fifty-five was no age to die. Not just her mum – anyone. Life was just so unfair sometimes.

If her mum was still alive, she'd tell Vogue what to do. Give her the strength to fight what she now thought was a losing battle. Vogue just didn't know whether or not she wanted to continue. It all felt so worthless. And who was to say, if Vogue survived this drama, she'd be strong enough to face another one when it came up.

Vogue could almost hear her mum telling her to stop talking like a quitter, but all that did was add to the heaviness already weighing down her heart. It was times like this, she wished she had a partner to lean on. Someone to take half the weight. Reassure her that things were going to turn out okay. Instead, as always, she was alone.

A voice from behind her caused her to turn around and look straight into the eyes of an elderly woman, who looked to be in her eighties.

'I've been watching you for a while.'

Vogue stood up, not knowing how to respond to her comment and even if she should.

'This place brings it all home, doesn't it?' The woman continued, 'Makes you wonder what it's all about. One minute we're young and free, then before you know it, you're my age and left wondering where all the time went.'

Vogue wasn't even near her forties, yet she could understand where the woman was coming from. It felt like life had passed by in a blink of an eye these past ten years. One minute she was twenty, and before she looked around, she was thirty. If the next few years went as quickly as those, it wouldn't be long before she was middle-aged.

The question was, would she still be single? Lonely? Fighting to swim upstream to keep her business alive? Who knew? And at that moment in time, she really didn't care.

'Do you mind if I sit?' The woman said, slowly shuffling along the path towards the bench.

Vogue moved aside, offering her arm as support as the woman slowly lowered herself onto the bench.

'What's your name?'

'Vogue.'

'I'm Elsie.'

Vogue smiled. 'Nice to meet you, Elsie.'

Elsie gestured to the grave. 'Your mother?'

Vogue took a seat beside her. 'Yes.'

'She was very young.'

Vogue sighed but said nothing.

'You know my biggest regret in life? Worrying. It stole the happiness I should've had.' Elsie shook her head. 'My ma used to always say "don't worry about things that might happen today or tomorrow, enjoy every second like it's your last". I wish I would've listened to her. It would've saved a lot of heartbreak in my life.'

'In what way?'

'Oh, too many ways to count.' Elsie looked thoughtful. 'I spent too much time worrying if people liked me, what they thought about me, fitting in… then as you get older and wiser, you begin to realise that most of the time the people who you thought were judging you, were too busy thinking about themselves. I'm sure they didn't give me a second thought.'

Elsie laughed, then continued, 'How's that for a wake-up call? But by then it's too late for some people to start again in the hope of following their dreams. They're either too jaded or they end up here. I often wonder how many people come here with their dreams still in them. How many were too scared to be their best because they were worried about other people?'

'Did you follow your dream, Elsie?'

Elsie's little mouth drooped in sadness, and tears brimmed in her eyes. 'No. I always wanted to travel the world, but too many bad choices prevented that from happening. I haven't even been on a plane despite renewing my passport every ten years. Silly, isn't it?'

'Not at all.'

Vogue looked around the cemetery, Elsie's words still on her mind. Is that what she wanted? When she took her last breath, to be filled with regret for all the things she was too scared to do?

So what if her company failed. She would build another one. So what if she never found love. She could love herself. Elsie was right. What was the point of worrying? There wasn't any. All she could do was give life her best shot, and whatever cards she was dealt, she would play them to the best of her ability.

Vogue jumped to her feet, feeling like she had been given a second lifeline.

'Elsie, I can't thank you enough for this talk.' She leant over and kissed her on the top of her head. 'I hope to see you again.'

Elsie smiled. 'I'm here every day. Over there.'

'I'll see you soon then!'

If Elsie wasn't so fragile, Vogue would have swept her up in her arms and squeezed her as tight as she could.

Instead, she flashed Elsie a grateful smile and ran the short distance to her car.

Thankfully, the traffic to the office wasn't too bad and she made it in record time.

When the lift took too long to reach the ground floor, Vogue took the stairs, climbing them two at a time until she reached the second floor. Without thinking about what she was going to say or how she was going to say it, she burst into the office and went straight to Amelia's desk.

Amelia looked up at her startled, as if she was overwhelmed with Vogue's burst of energy.

'I need you to come to my office.'

'I—'

'Right now, and bring your designs with you.'

Amelia said nothing as she slowly got to her feet.

She picked up her sketchpad and fell into line beside Vogue as she headed towards the door.

When they were in the lift alone, it was then Vogue sensed Amelia's apprehension. Noticing that she was having difficulty looking her in the eye.

'Something wrong?' Vogue asked.

'No, I mean….' Amelia fidgeted with the sketchpad she held in her hand. 'I'm just a bit surprised. I know I don't know you very well, but I didn't expect you to be… like this.'

'And how should I be? I feel great.'

Amelia stared at her. 'So, is it true?'

'Eh?' Vogue asked, completely unaware of what Amelia was talking about.

'You haven't heard? The tweet?'

The lift doors opened and neither woman made any attempt to leave.

'What tweet?'

Before Amelia had the chance to answer, Vogue's phone rang. It was Tina.

'Hey, Tina, guess—'

'I'm sorry, Vogue, I have to retract my offer.'

'But—'

'This is out of my hands. I'm sorry.'

The line went dead. No explanation. No nothing.

'That was the distributor… I am so fucked!'

Amelia reached over and pressed the button to the ground floor. 'You look like you need a drink.'

All Vogue could do was nod her head in complete compliance. 'I need to go home.'

Chapter Twenty-Nine

Amelia could see the pain etched in Vogue's features. Her skin so pale as if the blood had been drained from her body. Vogue still hadn't answered her question about whether or not the tweet was true, but she didn't need to. In her heart, Amelia knew there was another explanation.

Vogue was not a thief. She had absolutely no reason to steal someone else's work. The student she paid off or Trudy's design.

If that had been the case, she could easily have taken Amelia's, but she hadn't. She saw the way Vogue openly praised other designers. There was nothing covert about her interactions with people. If the designers were happy to share their ideas with others, Vogue actively encouraged it. That wasn't the sign of a woman who stole people's ideas. It pissed her off that Melissa hadn't been up front with her at the start. It would have meant Amelia wouldn't have made up crazy stories in her head about Vogue being a big bad wolf.

Vogue still looked in a daze as she opened the door to her house and gestured for Amelia to enter first.

Looking around, Amelia had to suppress the urge to give a low whistle at the place. It was one of the nicest homes she'd ever been in. The muted and subtle décor made the expanse of the place look less showy and more stylish.

Vogue led the way to the kitchen and to Amelia's

surprise, took out a bottle of water, not the wine that was right next to it.

Unscrewing the lid, Vogue spoke for the first time since leaving the office. 'You want something stronger?'

Amelia shook her head. 'I'll have a tea if you don't mind.'

Vogue flipped on the kettle and took a mug from one of the cupboards.

'I thought it would be you needing something stronger,' Amelia said.

'What's the point? Drinking isn't going to do anything other than give me a bad hangover.' Vogue hesitated. 'I'm going to change into something more comfortable. Won't be a minute.'

Amelia didn't know whether or not to bring up the tweet again, and what it meant for her future. All morning the office had been abuzz with rumours of Styles probably having to close their doors, due to the wave of bad publicity the tweet had garnered.

But now that Amelia thought about it, there was something that wasn't sitting quite right with her. When she had arrived at work that morning, she had thought things would be awkward between herself and Jordan, or at least there be a little tension, but to her surprise, Jordan had seemed pleased to see her. That wasn't what was bothering her though. It was the fact that Jordan had asked her if she'd changed her mind on her proposal.

When Amelia had informed her that she hadn't, Jordan had said she'd better think again, as if she knew the shit was about to hit the fan.

Was Jordan responsible for telling someone about the theft of Trudy's designs? The same person who tweeted about the one million pounds Vogue had paid to keep things quiet. Is that how Jordan knew it was all going to kick off?

Amelia debated whether she should tell Vogue or not. If she was wrong, she could get Jordan into trouble. But if she said nothing and Jordan was somehow involved with the leak of information, Vogue needed to know. If Amelia didn't, what else would Jordan end up doing?

Amelia made herself a cup of tea and walked around the kitchen, taking in the cookbooks and photos on the wall. It was a nice atmosphere and she could imagine herself living in a place like this. Big, spacious and airy.

One photo in particular caught her attention. A strikingly beautiful woman holding the cutest baby she'd ever seen. *Obviously Vogue.*

Amelia jumped when she heard Vogue's voice behind her.

'So you found my embarrassing baby picture.'

'Embarrassing? You're gorgeous, ahem,' Amelia quickly added, 'I mean as a baby. I take it she's your mum? I can see where you get your looks from. Does she still look hot, I mean good?'

'I don't think so, being a corpse and all.'

Amelia covered her mouth with her hand. 'Oh my God, I'm so sorry. I didn't realise.'

'It's okay, you weren't to know.'

Amelia sat down at the dining table and Vogue followed. She'd changed out of her suit into a pair of jeans and a white shirt.

'Has it been long?'

'A year,' Vogue said, 'but it seems like yesterday.'

'I can't even begin to imagine.'

'Yeah, it's tough, but it's just something you have to live with. It's going to happen to us all one day. Anyway, I've got more pressing things on my mind. Like the fact that someone's trying to ruin me.'

'Looks that way,' Amelia agreed. 'But do you have any idea why?'

Vogue shook her head. 'I have an idea of who it might be, but I don't understand why she wants to hurt me.'

'Jealousy?' Amelia said.

'I doubt it. We were business partners. Equal split, fifty-fifty. If anything, she got way more attention than me.'

'Did you piss her off?'

At this Vogue smiled and Amelia melted.

'Like I pissed you off?'

'You haven't pissed me off.'

'No?' Vogue said raising her eyebrows.

'What makes you think that?'

'Because I wasn't very responsive when you opened up to me. To be honest, I was shocked that someone with your talent could feel like that.'

'You know what they say about judging a book by

its cover,' Amelia said, unconsciously stroking the back of her neck.

'Yeah, but I'm sorry if I hurt you. I know it must've taken a lot to be so open.'

Amelia gave a nervous laugh. 'I forgive you.'

'Does that mean you're going to stop avoiding me like the plague.'

'I haven't,' Amelia said.

'You have so.'

'Well, it's not been intentional.'

'So what has it been?'

'Hold on a second, how have we moved from trying to work out who has it in for you, to me ignoring you?'

'It's just a natural flow of conversation.' Vogue smiled. 'You got a problem with that?'

'No...' *Yes I have!*

'So tell me, if you're not keeping me at arm's length intentionally, what's the problem?'

'Well, you're my boss for a start.'

Vogue laughed. 'I might not be for much longer.'

'Don't say that.'

'It's true. If I can't talk Tina 'round there's not a chance in hell my company will survive this.'

'Then you'll just have to make sure you persuade her.'

'You're very sure of yourself, aren't you?'

'No... I'm just sure of you.'

Vogue reached over and took Amelia's hand in her own. 'That's very kind of you.'

'It's true,' Amelia said, trying to keep her voice steady.

When Vogue removed her hand, the heat still lingered. If she wouldn't have looked so desperate, Amelia would have asked Vogue to kiss her. To take her to wherever her bedroom was and do whatever she wanted to do with her. More than anything, she just wanted to remove the underlying tension that resided between them. It was becoming unbearable to maintain a façade of not wanting her.

'What are you thinking about?'

'You.' The word left Amelia's mouth before she could stop herself.

'What about me?'

'I… I….' Amelia's brain froze. What if Vogue laughed at her? Rejected her?

'You?' Vogue pressed, keeping her eyes trained on Amelia's lips.

Amelia tried to work out her options. She knew exactly where this moment was leading as Vogue brought her chair closer.

Amelia could back off and voice her concerns out loud. Tell Vogue that she didn't want to cross the line with her boss. *Even though that's a load of bullshit. I'd cross any line to be with her.*

No, she wouldn't do that. No way. So what choice was left? To simply give into her desires and let fate lead the way… or just leave.

Before she knew what she was doing, Amelia stood. Vogue looked as shocked as she felt.

'I'd better get back to the office.'

'Why? It's not like you're going to get in trouble with the boss.' Vogue started to get up but stopped midway when Amelia gestured for her to sit back down.

If Vogue came anywhere near her, Amelia knew she wouldn't be able to resist her.

It was bad enough just being alone in her house with her, knowing that somewhere in the vicinity there was a bed that they could both be cavorting on – naked!

Oh fuck, I've got to get out of here.

Amelia laughed nervously. 'It doesn't matter, I've still got work to do on my designs.'

'Okay, fair enough.' Vogue slumped back in her seat. The forlorn expression on her face made Amelia want to go and hold her until the look was replaced with one of happiness and contentment.

Amelia suddenly felt sorry for her. Feeling the need to fix the problem and sympathising with Vogue's situation, she came up with a solution.

'How about we meet at BH1 later,' Amelia said, hoping she wasn't going to regret her sudden weakness.

Okay, so Amelia knew she was going against everything she'd said but Vogue really did look like she needed support. That was the least she could do. It wasn't as if she was playing favourites, she would reach out to anyone going through a hard time.

Vogue's face brightened at this suggestion.

'Great, I'll get a cab instead of driving.'

'Good idea.' Amelia backed away, still not trusting herself to not do or say something she might regret.

'Well, I'll see you later then.'

'Yes, you will.'

Once safely inside the Uber, Amelia could have kicked herself. How could she have walked away from such an opportunity. They had been so close to…. *Grrr, I'm such an idiot!*

Images of what they could have been doing swept through her imagination and she had to force herself to keep her eyes open to stop the raging fantasy.

Twenty minutes later, she was behind her desk again, still trying to focus. Still trying to get Vogue out of her mind. On both counts she was failing miserably.

'Where'd you disappear to?'

Amelia looked up to see Jordan staring at her, flustered she said, 'For a walk. I needed some air.'

Jordan eyed her suspiciously before sitting on the edge of her desk. 'So you haven't heard the latest?'

Amelia shook her head.

'Seems all this has been for nothing.'

'How come?'

'The company that Vogue had her eye on for her outwear collection pulled out.'

'How'd you know?' Amelia said. Her longing for Vogue had sapped her energy so it didn't take much to pretend that she didn't know. *But how does Jordan know?* They were alone in the lift when Vogue received the call from the distribution company.

Unless someone told her. But who? To find that out, she'd have to ask Vogue who she'd spoken to. And that wouldn't happen until she met up with her later.

Damn! Amelia was intrigued by this developing little drama. It would be interesting to see where it all led.

***

Sitting at a table at BH1, Vogue looked at Amelia in confusion. 'Are you sure that's what she said? You didn't mishear her?'

Amelia nodded while taking a mouthful of beer. 'I'm twenty-eight, Vogue, not ninety-eight. My hearing's just fine.'

'But it doesn't make any sense.'

'That's what I thought. So did you tell anyone else, apart from me, after I left your place?' Amelia asked. *This is what it must feel like being a detective. Trying to figure out where the parts of the puzzle fit.*

Vogue remained silent.

Oh my God, please say you did! The last thing she wanted was for Vogue to think she was responsible for spreading rumours about her business.

'I only told one person.'

Amelia said a silent prayer. *Thank you, God.*

'Who?'

'Melissa.'

'Melissa?' Amelia asked in confusion. 'Why would Melissa tell Jordan something as sensitive as that?'

Vogue shrugged. 'I have no idea.'

'I mean, it's not like they even really know each other.'

'I don't get it either,' Vogue said, looking visibly defeated. 'She probably said it in passing. I'm sure it wasn't done intentionally. Anyway, it's not as if me paying off that student wasn't going to come out one day. In a way, I'm glad it's all out in the open.'

'So do you know what you're going to do?'

'Get drunk and….'

Vogue looked at her and Amelia could tell exactly what she was thinking about. Because Amelia was having the exact thoughts.

'Do you want to come back to mine?' Vogue asked.

'To get drunk?'

'And more I hope,' Vogue said with a deep warmth in her eyes as she tilted her head to the side

'That's very direct.'

Vogue's eyes searched Amelia's and Amelia's heart fluttered. 'I'm tired of playing games.'

As she spoke, Cecile's warning to steer clear of Vogue niggled at the back of her mind but she immediately blocked it out with a voice of her own. A stronger, louder one. She was a grown woman for God's sake. If she wanted to sleep with someone, it was her business and her business alone. She didn't have to justify herself to anyone. Besides, it wasn't as if she was going to fall head over heels in love with Vogue after spending the night with her.

To her surprise, Vogue suddenly looked remorseful. 'Sorry, this probably isn't the best time to—'

'Yes, it is,' Amelia said, quickly hoping she hadn't

blown it. 'I'm tired of playing games too.'

'You are?' Vogue reached out and laid her hand on Amelia's thigh.

A tingling sensation ran through Amelia's veins at Vogue's touch. While she enjoyed the searing heat emanating from Vogue's hand right up between her legs, she glanced around the room to make sure no prying eyes were looking in their direction. She needn't have bothered. The other customers were too engrossed in their own conversations to be interested in what was going on between the two of them.

'Yes.'

It felt so good to be honest. To actually say what was on her mind instead of putting up a façade. Amelia wanted Vogue and it felt like a weight had been lifted off her heart now she'd finally been able to reveal the truth.

'Shall we go?' Vogue's hand moved a little further up Amelia's thigh.

The heat intense, Amelia glanced away again, suddenly feeling shy under Vogue's gaze. 'I thought you'd never ask.'

Amelia's stomach flipped as the result of Vogue's mischievous grin. She could only imagine what Vogue had in store for her. That's if they ever got out of the bar which didn't look like it was going to happen anytime soon. Melissa had just entered and spotted them immediately, waving over to Amelia as she walked to the bar, indicating she was going to get a round for them all.

Her heart sank. How long was it going to be before they could escape and retreat into their own little cocoon for the night? When she saw Melissa heading over to them with two bottles of wine, Amelia realised they were in for a wait.

'Hey, guys,' Melissa said, placing the bottles of wine and glasses down on the table.

'Hi, Melissa.' Amelia took the glass of wine Melissa held out to her.

'You okay?' Melissa said to Vogue as she took a seat next to her.

'Not really.' Vogue turned to her and the look of lust that had been present on her face only moments before was replaced with the sternness of a majorly pissed off boss.

'Why, what's up?'

If Melissa was nervous, she showed no sign of it.

'Did you tell anyone about the situation with Tina?'

Amelia studied Melissa closely, trying to read her body language.

'Of course not. Why would I?' Melissa said, slowly looking away from Vogue to Amelia and back again.

'Well, someone in the office knows and it sure as hell wasn't me that told them.'

'So you think it was me?'

'You're the only one who knew.'

Melissa looked aggrieved. 'You know something, Vogue, I've just about had it with your shit.'

Melissa slammed her glass on the table, causing the

liquid to flow over the rim.

Though her reaction wasn't in proportion to what Vogue said, Amelia had a feeling that Melissa's words were a long time coming. The pent-up anger was plain to see.

Vogue's eyes widened. 'What're you talking about?'

'You! And your fucking paranoia. Always thinking someone's got it in for you.' Melissa stood. 'Jordan could have heard it from anyone—'

'I—'

'You know what, Vogue, I'm done with this shit. Think what the fuck you want. I'm out of here.'

Melissa took off without another word, leaving both Amelia and Vogue to stare at one another.

It was Amelia that said what was on both their minds.

'How did she know you were talking about Jordan?'

'Because she obviously told her.' Vogue was on her feet. 'I'm sorry but we're going to have to do this another time.'

Vogue grabbed her jacket and ran towards the exit, leaving Amelia alone with nothing but two bottles of wine and an unfulfilled fantasy for company.

Chapter Thirty

Vogue stepped out of the bar, looking in all directions until she finally caught sight of Melissa hurrying across the road. Shoving her arms inside her jacket, Vogue took off in Melissa's direction, calling out after her as she did so.

'Melissa, wait!'

Melissa turned her head briefly and seeing Vogue, quickened her pace.

'Will you wait!' Vogue increased her speed until she was a few feet behind Melissa. 'Are you going to tell me what's going on?'

Melissa stopped and spun around. 'What's going on? Are you taking the piss?'

'I know you told Jordan, Melissa.'

Melissa looked at her incredulously. 'What? Who?'

'Are you going to lie straight to my face?'

'Lie about what? I told you the stress of all of this was going to get the better of you and it seems it finally has. Look at you... your business is going down the drain and you're in a bar trying to fuck one of your employees, and on top of that, you've got the fucking cheek to accuse me of something I didn't do—'

'I didn't mention Jordan's name.'

A flicker of confusion clouded Melissa's eyes. 'What?'

'I said I didn't tell you it was Jordan that knew.'

'Yes, you did. You said—'

'D'you want me to go and get Amelia? She heard exactly what you said.'

Looking like a deer caught in headlights, Melissa bowed her head. 'Yeah, okay, so I fucked up.'

'When did we start lying to each other?' Vogue took a step closer and Melissa backed away. 'I always thought we had each other's back.'

'We did, we do, look…' Melissa ran her fingers through her hair. 'All of this is just getting too much for me. I don't know what I'm doing anymore. Yes, I told Jordan, but it wasn't intentional, I was just thinking out loud and she overheard me.'

'So why didn't you just say?'

'You were reprimanding me like a child in front of Amelia. D'you know how embarrassing that is?'

Vogue saw the hurt in her face and immediately regretted not speaking to Melissa in private. She was right. It was out of order bringing it up in front of Amelia, but she hadn't been thinking straight. *That'll be my lust-filled brain.*

'I'm sorry, Mel. And you're right, I was bang out of order saying it in front of Amelia, but there's more to this than that, isn't there?'

Vogue wasn't stupid. She could read people. That was one of the many skills she had as a businesswoman. You had to learn to read people if you wanted to get ahead. And what she had seen in Melissa wasn't mere frustration, it was hatred. Full blown hatred. What she couldn't understand was why? After all they had been through together, the highs and lows, the successes and failures, she really did look at Melissa as a sister. Someone she would trust her life with. But seeing that look in her eyes, made Vogue question if she really ever knew Melissa at all. The worst thing was that Melissa didn't even try to hide it.

'No, you're right. I'm sick of being treated like I'm nothing. That I don't matter.'

'What do you mean? Of course you matter—'

'Only when it fucking suits you. When you need a pick me up, or need someone to go and do your running around like a skivvy.'

'That's not true.'

'Isn't it? When was the last time you asked me how I was feeling? How I was dealing with this mess you got us into?'

So she does blame me for what Bev put us through. I can't believe it.

'You never listen to a word I say, ever. You just use me like an old toy, play with me one minute, then throw me to the side as soon as something new comes along to take your attention. I mean, you even had to go after Amelia, didn't you? Knowing that I liked her—'

Vogue's eyes widened. 'I didn't know.'

'Oh, like hell you didn't. That's all you've ever done, take from me. Take, take, take, you even took our—' Melissa paused abruptly, snapping her mouth shut.

'Go on, you might as well get it all out while you're in the swing of things.'

'Forget it,' Melissa said, her shoulders slumping

like life had been knocked out of her. 'It doesn't matter anymore.' Melissa turned and started to walk off again.

'We need to talk,' Vogue called after her.

'That's just it. We really don't.'

Melissa reached her car and got inside. Several seconds later, she took off into the darkness.

Vogue turned in the direction of the bar and seeing Amelia suddenly appear, Vogue knew what she wanted. To forget about everything and lose herself in the woman she'd slowly been falling in love with.

***

The drive back to her house had been a silent one. Not because there was an awkwardness between them, but because there was nothing for either of them to say. They knew what was going to take place once they closed the door behind them, and by the way Vogue caught Amelia looking at her, she knew Amelia wanted it as much as she did.

When they entered the house, Vogue reached for the light, only to be stopped by Amelia as she pulled Vogue up against her.

Heart thundering hard, Vogue pinned Amelia to the door, pressing her arms above her head as she leant in and claimed her mouth. Gently at first, she then applied more pressure as she slid her tongue between Amelia's open lips. Invading her more deeply as Vogue's hands slid down Amelia's front, roughly tugging her shirt from her jeans before finding her erect nipple beneath the fabric of her bra.

Amelia let out a gasp, gripping Vogue's arse tightly as she pulled her closer, grinding her leg between Vogue's thighs.

Vogue bit Amelia's earlobe delicately as she whispered, 'Are you sure this is what you want?'

Amelia pulled back and gazed at Vogue. The intensity of her stare was enough of a reply.

Too impatient to make it to the bedroom, Vogue sank onto the hardwood floor and gently pulled Amelia down with her, sweeping kisses across her collarbone as Amelia lay beneath her on the dark oak floor. Amelia's body arched into Vogue's as they ground their pelvises together.

This wasn't how Vogue had wanted their first time to be but the need, the urgency to touch Amelia, taste her, was overwhelming. She would make up for it later, but for now there was no stopping the momentum.

In the darkness, she could hear Amelia's breath quicken as Vogue unbuttoned her shirt, sliding her hand under Amelia's bra and massaging her firm breast, enjoying the start Amelia gave at her touch. Vogue loved the texture of Amelia's skin under her hand – smooth, soft.

Pushing away the fabric, Vogue lowered her mouth and captured Amelia's erect nipple between her teeth, gently biting, sucking and teasing Amelia as she squirmed beneath her. Amelia's fingers threaded through Vogue's hair as Vogue slowly made her way down her body, tugging Amelia's jeans and underwear off when reaching her waist. Vogue wanted nothing more than to get her mouth between Amelia's thighs, to taste her.

Vogue parted Amelia's legs, spreading them wide as she pressed her mouth against Amelia's smooth and bare centre, her juices causing Vogue's tongue to slip and slide as it flicked around the pink, swollen clit. Amelia lifted her hips up to Vogue's face, moaning.

Vogue pulled away, teasing Amelia as she did so. 'So wet already?'

The breath left Vogue's lungs in a ragged rush. Her nipples ached they were so hard, her own clit throbbing as Amelia rocked her hips to meet Vogue's tongue.

Amelia's thigh muscles jerked as Vogue slipped two fingers into Amelia's slit, the channel clenching around them tightly, holding them captive. Vogue's heartbeat gained speed with every thrust. She continued to flick Amelia's clit with her tongue as her fingers gently increased momentum.

'Fuck me harder,' Amelia begged.

Vogue glanced up to Amelia's flushed face, her words igniting a fire inside Vogue she'd never experienced before. Her own climax was near despite the lack of contact.

Vogue slipped in another finger and thrust hard inside Amelia, pulling her mouth away from Amelia's clit in order to achieve more force. Vogue watched Amelia groan and writhe beneath her as Vogue forced her fingers deep inside. Amelia's back arched in anticipation of her approaching climax and Vogue immediately returned to her clit, lapping hard as Amelia cried out, her legs trembling.

Kissing her way up Amelia's limp body, Vogue stopped to take her time with each nipple, up one side of her neck and finally to her ear.

'This is just the beginning…'

***

Amelia lay on the cold wooden floor, unable to move.

Is this really happening? Have I actually had sex for the first time in a year? And with Vogue!

Vogue's voice broke into her thoughts before she could pinch herself.

'Shall we go to the bedroom? You must be freezing,' Vogue whispered, her fingers caressing Amelia's abdomen.

'I'm not sure I can move.'

Vogue smiled and kissed her gently on the lips.

I've well and truly crossed the line now. Amelia knew there was no coming back from this.

Vogue got to her feet, helped Amelia up then led her through to the bedroom.

Large bay windows let in the moonlight which cast a pale white streak over the super king-sized bed that dominated the room.

Amelia stepped out of the shadow and climbed onto the bed, her hands and knees sinking into the softness of the feather-filled duvet as she quickly removed her bra and shirt. Eager and waiting with anticipation, she stared at Vogue who stood at the foot of the bed, looking back at her as she stripped down to her underwear.

Vogue bent to crawl onto the bed, but Amelia stopped her with a slight raise of her hand.

'No, take the rest off. I want to see you.'

Everything faded away. The soft moonlight highlighted Vogue's figure beautifully as she dropped her bra and panties seductively to the floor.

She is so amazing. Goose pimples erupted all over Amelia's body as she drank in the swell of Vogue's breasts. Her desire for this woman was a never-ending ache in her body.

Despite just having the most powerful orgasm ever, Amelia's clit began to throb once again. The excitement building inside her.

She beckoned Vogue towards her. Her chest expanding with each breath she took. This time she was going to take charge. Amelia was not submissive when it came to sex, she never had been. Although her self-esteem was low outside of the bedroom, when it came to getting satisfaction sexually, she was another person altogether.

'Touch yourself,' Amelia said to Vogue who now lay next to her.

Vogue slid her hand down between her thighs, rubbing gently with her gaze fixed directly on Amelia.

Amelia lay there watching, waiting. Waiting for the right moment to touch Vogue, to send her over the edge. As Vogue's rhythm increased, Amelia reached out and caressed her breast, circling Vogue's nipple with her finger. She squeezed gently, and a gasp escaped Vogue's lips. Amelia moved towards her, covering Vogue's mouth with her own and kissing her deeply. Her hand trailed its way along the curve of Vogue's body and down between her legs. Amelia's fingers entered her, Vogue still playing with her own clit.

Vogue groaned against Amelia's lips, her excitement more and more evident with every thrust.

Amelia stopped abruptly, gesturing for Vogue to straddle her. Vogue changed position, lowering her wetness into Amelia's eager mouth. Vogue rode Amelia's tongue, her hand firmly placed on the wall in front of her.

Amelia had never experienced such intensity before. Never had the taste of a woman sent her to such heights. As her tongue continued to flick Vogue's clit, Vogue's breathing became rapid, and Amelia delved deep inside her which was enough to send Vogue over. Amelia continued to suck and lick as Vogue's juices flowed. Vogue slumped forward, unable to take anymore, but Amelia held her in place still teasing until the very end.

Vogue slid down on top of Amelia, their bodies entwined, their breasts pressed together, hips and thighs melting into one.

'All I can say is oh my God,' Vogue said, still breathless.

Amelia smiled to herself. It was good to know that after a year of celibacy she hadn't lost her touch.

Chapter Thirty-One

Melissa's hand trembled so uncontrollably, she could barely hold her phone in her hand.

'What the fuck did you do? You nearly landed me right in it.'

Jordan's voice was apologetic. 'I'm sorry, Melissa, I didn't even think.'

'That's the problem, you never do.' Melissa pressed the phone hard against her ear, half wishing she could somehow travel down the line and see Jordan face-to-face.

'So how did you talk yourself out of it?' Jordan asked casually which only served to wind Melissa up even further. Jordan was oblivious to how close she was to being caught out by Vogue.

'By causing a distraction. Turning the blame back onto her.' As Melissa spoke, she recalled how easily Vogue had bought her explanation.

'So what's next?'

There wasn't anything next for Jordan. Her part in this project was over. She was too much of a liability. This time Melissa had managed to escape by the skin of her teeth, next time she might not be so lucky. Vogue wouldn't be so gullible if she fucked up again.

'I want you to email your resignation tomorrow, effective immediately. Stating, in light of the latest revelation, you can't work with a company you can't trust, blah, blah, blah.'

'Okay. It's a shame 'cause I really enjoyed working there. If you ever need my help again, you know where I am.'

'Sure do,' Melissa said, knowing full well that was the last contact she would be making with Jordan ever again.

She could have ruined everything by not keeping her mouth closed. And to tell Amelia of all people. The stupidity of the woman knew no bounds.

Agitated beyond belief, Melissa knocked back a mouthful of brandy and winced as the liquid burnt her throat. This was unravelling too fast for her. She hadn't expected her tweet to go viral straight away. What had made things worse was seeing Amelia and Vogue together. The connection between them was undeniable and she knew there was no way she was going to be able to draw Amelia away from her. Once Vogue got her claws into someone, unless she dumped them, they never wanted to leave.

Melissa picked up the only picture she had of her mother, given to her by her adoptive parents when they sprung the news on her. For twenty-one years she had grown up believing Mike and Polly were her parents, even considering how odd their whole family dynamics were. For starters, she looked nothing like either of them. Not the slightest bit of a resemblance. Even strangers noticed. She could remember several times when people had been surprised that Polly was her mum. Melissa had ignored her gut feeling despite knowing deep down something was wrong. But how could she have ever known, guessed the truth? That they would have lied to her for so many years?

Ever since Melissa walked out of their door, she had not looked back. The one time she had seen Polly in the street, Melissa had walked past her as if she was a stranger. Because in reality, that's what she was. They weren't related, and they certainly didn't have anything in common. It was then she went in search of her biological mother, only to find out that she had another daughter.

What was so wrong with her that her own mother rejected her? It must have been bad considering she kept Vogue – the golden girl.

It was strange that Melissa hadn't wanted to bond with her like a sister would have. There was something about her, this sense of entitlement that always made her keep Vogue at arm's length. That invisible barrier that repelled her. It was an instinctive move. A protection of some sort to keep her safe. But it was pointless. Nothing made Melissa feel safe. Not after knowing the people that were supposed to have loved her had lied for most of her life.

What normal sane person could feel safe after that?

Chapter Thirty-Two

Amelia awoke and was relieved to see she was in Vogue's bedroom and not at home. If she had been, the previous night would have been nothing but a dream. Thankfully, life hadn't been that cruel. Flashbacks to a few hours earlier caused a prolonged tingling sensation between her thighs. The highs Vogue had taken her to had been well worth the year-long drought. In fact, if she never had sex for the rest of her natural life, Amelia was quite happy to live off the many memories she had stored in her brain.

Vogue stirred beside her and for a moment she was overcome with 'Morning shyness' as she called it. The moment you had to face the woman who had heard you saying things that would normally be kept safely locked away in your head.

'Morning,' Vogue said.

Hearing the smile in her voice, Amelia rolled onto her side to face her. 'Morning yourself. How long've you been awake?'

Vogue pushed away a lock of hair that had fallen across Amelia's eye. 'About twenty minutes.'

'What've you been doing?'

Vogue smiled. 'Looking at your neck.'

'Really?' Amelia said, unconsciously resting her hand on her neck.

'Yes, really, it's beautiful.'

'You're beautiful,' Amelia said unable to tear her

eyes from Vogue's face.

Vogue frowned. 'Even with bags under my eyes?'

'I couldn't care less what you look like.' Amelia placed the palm of her hand on Vogue's heart area. 'It's what's in there what matters.'

Vogue covered Amelia's hand with her own and smiled. 'I'm going to take that as a compliment. Has anyone ever told you how sweet you are?'

'Hmm, let me think, sweet? No.' Amelia inched forward and snuggled up close against Vogue. 'And if I recall, you weren't calling me sweet last night.'

Vogue laughed. 'And what was I calling you?'

'Hot, horny, wet, ho—'

Vogue burst out laughing, covering Amelia's mouth with her hand. 'I did not call you a ho.'

Amelia joined in with her laughter. 'Did too.'

'I have never used that word in my life.'

'Yeah, I was just kidding.' Amelia tilted Vogue's face up and kissed her. 'I don't want to get up.'

'Who said you have to?' Vogue said, wrapping her arms around Amelia.

'Me. I promised Cecile I'd go shopping with her today. She's got a date.'

'Nice,' Vogue nuzzled Amelia's neck. 'Who is she?'

'She?' Amelia drew back slightly, wondering why Vogue would say such an odd thing. 'Cecile isn't into women.'

'She could've fooled me.'

'What does that mean?' Amelia asked, immediately noticing the change in the atmosphere.

'Nothing, forget I said anything.'

'Come on, Vogue, you can't make a comment like that and just brush it off.'

'Look, if she hasn't told you, it isn't my place to.'

'Told me what?' Amelia said exasperated. She hated it when people didn't just get straight to the point. It drove her crazy. 'I wish you'd stop talking in riddles.'

Vogue sighed as she rolled out of bed and slipped into a shirt.

'This really isn't the kind of conversation we should be having after we just slept with each other,' Vogue said, glancing over her shoulder at Amelia who had now pushed herself into a sitting position.

'I think this is exactly the time to be honest with each other.' Amelia tried to keep the edge out of her voice but failed miserably.

'Fine.' Vogue threw her hands in the air. 'You want to know the truth? I slept with Cecile.'

Amelia burst out laughing and attempted to pull Vogue down onto the bed. 'Okay, if you don't want to tell me, I'll respect your wishes.'

Vogue resisted and instead stood and turned to look at her. 'It's the truth, Amelia.'

'You and Cecile?' Amelia frowned. Not quite sure she'd heard right. 'But… she's… she's straight.'

Vogue shrugged and started towards the en-suite. 'I'm just telling you as it is. I'm going to take a shower.'

'Wait! Is this what you do then? Work your way through the office? Am I just another notch on your bedpost?'

Vogue turned around, anger flashing in her eyes. 'I am not even going to dignify that with a response.'

Vogue disappeared into the en-suite whilst Amelia got out of bed and went in search of her clothes. Vogue's words raced around her mind as she tried to make sense of it. *Vogue and Cecile?* How could she trust either of them again?

Amelia needed to speak to Cecile and find out what the hell she was playing at.

***

As Amelia stood at the front door searching for her keys in her bag, her phone rang but she ignored it. She didn't want anything to distract her from what she was going to say. It was going to be straight to the point and she hoped Cecile had a good reason for lying to her because if she didn't, Amelia didn't think she could continue with their friendship. Honesty was paramount to her, and it was the one value that she didn't back down on.

Entering the flat, Amelia kicked off her shoes and went in search of Cecile. She found her in the living room, sitting on the sofa, engrossed in the TV. She barely looked up when Amelia entered.

'We need to talk.' Amelia took the remote control and turned the TV off, then got straight to the point. 'Why did you lie to me about Vogue?'

'Lie? In what way?' Cecile's features were bland and expressionless.

'Oh, don't play the clueless card with me, Cecile.'

Cecile looked up at her with disdain. 'She told you

then? Was this before or after you fucked?'

'Does it matter?'

'Well, I'd hope any decent woman would tell someone they'd slept with their best friend before shagging them, wouldn't you?'

'Maybe she thought you'd already told me. What with you supposedly being my best friend and all?' Amelia said. She recognised Cecile's familiar features. Her voice. Just not the person.

Cecile gave her an awkward smile. 'Supposedly? Are you saying I'm not?'

'What kind of best friend lies? Why couldn't you just've been honest with me?' The thought entered Amelia's mind to leave before she ended up saying something she might regret. If she did, that could signal the end of their friendship. While Amelia didn't want anything that drastic to happen, she had to make Cecile understand that this wasn't something they could just sweep under the carpet and pretend like it never happened.

'I lied because I was ashamed,' Cecile said, bowing her head slightly.

"Cause you slept with a woman? There's nothing—'

'No, not because of that!' Cecile looked up again, meekness replaced with fire in her eyes. 'That bitch dumped me like I was a piece of trash. I know what she's like, Amelia. I just didn't want her to do the same thing to you.'

'So why not just come out and say it? All that rubbish you fed me about her were lies. She's nothing like you said she was. You were just pissed off 'cause she rejected you.'

'And you think she's not going to do the same to you? I know you think you're different, but you ain't nothing special.'

'Maybe not. But the one thing I'm not and never will be is deceitful.'

'Oh, get the fuck off your high horse. She'll break you, mark my words.'

'Why would I believe you? At the moment, I don't think I'll be able to do that ever again.'

'Always the dramatic one, eh?'

'No, I'm not. I'm just a realist. Anyway, I have to get ready for work. I'll see you later.'

Amelia headed for her room, berating herself for being such a trustworthy fool. How could she not have known what Cecile was up to? All that bitching and putting her down for even talking to Vogue, when all along she just wanted her for herself. Amelia wouldn't have minded if Cecile would have just been up front with her. If she had, Amelia would have totally backed off. Now they faced losing their friendship over a woman. It was a situation Amelia had never considered before. She thought her best friend was as straight as a line. In all the years she had known Cecile, she had never let it slip once that she was attracted to women. If she could hide that, what else was she hiding?

It was too early in the morning to have so much drama, Amelia would have to deal with it later.

Arriving at work, Amelia was surprised to see

Jordan's seat at her desk empty. She was normally the first there and the last to leave.

'Hey, Trudy, where's Jordan?'

'No idea,' Trudy said.

Hmm that's strange. She unlocked her drawer and took out her pad. Looking down at the design, she wondered if Vogue had fired her. But for what reason? She didn't have to wait long for her answer.

Melissa walked into the office with an expression that said she was there to announce bad news.

'Just thought I'd let you guys know, Jordan has resigned. She no longer felt Styles was a fit for her in light of recent events.'

Did she really jump or was she pushed?

'Is someone going to replace her?' Amelia asked when the others returned to their work.

'No.' Melissa took a seat by her side, speaking in a lowered tone so no one else could hear her. 'Considering the current situation, we don't think it would be appropriate to hire anyone else until we know where we stand with things.'

'Makes sense,' Amelia said. 'Are you okay after yesterday? You were pretty upset.'

'Yeah, I'm fine. Thanks for asking. Suppose everything's just getting a bit stressful. We've sorted our differences out.'

'Good, I only wish it was that easy for me and Cecile.'

'Oh? What happened?'

'I won't bore you with the details.'

'Don't be silly, I'm more than happy to listen.'

Amelia didn't know if she was doing the right thing, but her gut instinct was telling her to just do it. If she was going to help Vogue, she needed to know what Melissa's intentions were. Friend or Foe.

Vogue was too close to the situation to be objective, but she wasn't. After the bombshell with Cecile, she didn't think anyone could be trusted. Especially the ones who were so forthcoming with advice.

'In that case, can we meet up after work? I don't fancy going back to her place.'

'Of course.' Melissa scribbled her address on a piece of paper and handed it to Amelia. 'Come 'round mine. I'll cook.'

'Sounds good. Thanks, Melissa.'

'No problem. It'll be nice to spend some time with you alone.'

Amelia smiled, hoping she wasn't reading too much into her comment. All she wanted was information.

Definitely nothing else.

Chapter Thirty-Three

Melissa was beside herself with joy and hope as she made her way to Vogue's office for the latest rounds of talks. Amelia agreeing to dinner was a sure sign that the door wasn't closed on that connection just yet. There was still an opportunity and she was in with a chance. All she had to do was play it cool and keep her mouth shut when it came to Vogue. She wanted Amelia to believe that she was supporting Vogue through her time of need. That her loyalty was unwavering.

Vogue was standing by the window when Melissa walked into the conference room. She could almost smell the fear as she took the last remaining seat at the table. Looking around at the people she had worked with for the past year gave her nothing but feelings of contempt. They had all brown-nosed Vogue and catered to her every whim. In her mind, they deserved what they had coming to them.

Maybe it was a lesson they needed to learn – to grow a backbone. To not rely on anyone. They would learn the hard way, just like she had.

'So I'll be upfront… things are not looking good.' Vogue turned away from the window to face them all. 'In fact, I can categorically say this is looking like the end of the road for Styles. I tried talking Tina around, but she's not interested in doing business with us. No one is.'

John slammed his fist down on the table startling

everyone, even Melissa.

'Who the fuck leaked it? How could someone do this to us?'

Melissa pressed her lips firmly together to stop them curling up into a snarl. That was exactly what she was talking about. The undying loyalty. Styles wasn't John's company. He was merely an employee, yet the way he spoke was as if he had a personal investment in it.

Melissa wasn't doing anything to him. Vogue was her target and only Vogue. If others got caught in the crossfire, so be it.

'I wish I knew, John, but I fear whoever it is, they aren't going to give up. And by us continuing, all it's going to do is fan the flames. I'm just scared it's going to have an adverse effect on your names if you don't get out now. You'll be given a month's pay. That's all I can do, as well as a glowing reference for what it's worth.'

Melissa relaxed back in her seat. This was much easier than she thought. She was almost disappointed that the crashing of Vogue's empire wasn't a tad more dramatic. She was on the verge of offering her sympathy to the team when things took a sudden turn she wasn't expecting.

'We aren't leaving, Vogue. We believe in you. We know you had nothing to do with stealing that woman's designs,' John said with determination. 'And we're going to fight to the end. So what if Tina won't help. We'll find someone else. Even if it means looking outside the UK.'

'Yeah.' Chrissie stood too. 'You've always supported

us and been there for us no matter how big or small our problems have been. D'you really think we'd abandon you when you need us most?'

'We're going to weather this storm,' Carol said. 'You know what people are like, next week their minds will be focused elsewhere.'

The muscles in Melissa's face tensed as she clenched her teeth. It was all she could do not to scream as one by one, each of the people around the table professed their loyalty to Vogue and her company. What was even more sickening was the way Vogue lapped it all up.

Eyes brimming with tears, Vogue stood at the head of the table thanking everyone for their support, her hands resting on her hips, resembling a superhero about to fight her latest battle.

But Vogue wasn't a superhero, and this was one battle she wasn't going to win.

***

Melissa set the table in her moderately sized kitchen. Candles, white porcelain plates, crystal glasses, the only thing missing were rose petals. Her intention was to invoke a romantic atmosphere to the evening without being overly obvious. Pouring herself another glass of wine, she took a mouthful before checking the food in the oven – moussaka.

The accompanying salad was ready, the wine chilled, all she needed now was Amelia.

Melissa hadn't seen her since she'd left her office earlier that morning as Melissa had been too busy taking orders from Vogue. Her instructions were to find as many manufacturers as she could in China and try to set up meetings for her. Of course, Melissa had only played lip service to her request and spent most of the day calling random numbers and having meaningless conversations. The main thing was that she looked busy.

As if they were going to find anything. Melissa wasn't stupid. She had covered her tracks so deeply they'd need a professional to reveal them. There was no way they could trace anything back to her. Jordan wasn't going to blab again either.

The doorbell rang and Melissa made her way into the hallway, checking her appearance in the mirror before opening the door to Amelia.

'I didn't know if you preferred red or white, so I bought both,' Amelia said.

Melissa pulled Amelia in for a hug, trying not to linger for too long despite not wanting to let her go. 'Either's good, thanks.'

Melissa gestured for Amelia to follow her into the kitchen.

'Mmm, something smells good,' Amelia said, sniffing the air.

'I hope you like moussaka?'

'Love it. One of my favourite dishes.'

Amelia took her jacket off and handed it to Melissa, who hung it on the back of a chair.

'So how was your day?' Amelia asked as Melissa

plated their food.

'Manic.'

'Yeah, I noticed a lot of activity going on,' Amelia said.

'Did Vogue tell you her plans?'

Amelia shook her head.

'Oh, I thought she would have. You two seem to have got close.'

'Close? Not really? I only went out for a drink with her yesterday to talk about my designs and whether I wanted to jump ship.'

Melissa carried their food across the room to the dining table and Amelia followed.

It gave her a few seconds to figure things out in her mind. So, Vogue hadn't taken Amelia into her confidence like Melissa had first thought. That was a good sign.

'Oh right.' Melissa refilled their glasses.

'So I take it the news of the theft and plagiarism was the big secret you mentioned the other day?'

Melissa nodded. 'But it wasn't that much of a secret in the company. Most people higher up knew what had happened,' Melissa said, setting the scene to make others look liable for the leak. It wouldn't look good on her if Amelia thought she was the only person who knew what Vogue had been accused of.

'It must be hard for Vogue to face the industry with everyone thinking she's a thief. I mean, who would do something that evil? So hateful?'

'You make a lot of enemies in the business world.

It's dog eat dog.'

'I just don't understand why she paid the woman off.'

Melissa shrugged non-committedly. 'Who knows. Vogue and Bev were best friends, they were as thick as thieves, excuse the pun. Only they know what went down.'

Amelia snorted. 'Friend? I'm beginning to wonder if anyone is actually who they say they are.'

Melissa concentrated on her food, afraid of Amelia discovering the deception in her eyes.

'I think there's a lot more good people in this world than bad. It's just about weeding them out.'

'You think?' Amelia said, savouring a mouthful of food before taking a long sip of wine.

'Yes, I do.'

'So why d'you think someone would try to take Vogue down? Because that's what they're doing.'

'I have no idea.'

'So how did you know this was about to blow up?'

'People talk?'

'Like who?'

Melissa placed her cutlery on her plate. 'You seem very invested in this situation.'

'That's because I am. I don't want to be associated with a company whose boss steals from people. If there's any truth behind all of this, I'm ready to walk.'

The words hung in the air between them.

'You are?' Melissa asked.

'Of course. I hate the fact that people with money

are allowed to get away with things us mere mortals would probably be locked up for.'

'Totally agree with you on that,' Melissa said, thinking of the inheritance her mother left to Vogue. Every single last penny, without a thought in the world for Melissa. Not that Melissa wanted any of it, well what was left anyway.

All she wanted was recognition from the woman who brought her into the world, and she was denied that. What sort of a person did something like that?

'How's your food?' Melissa asked after a few minutes of silence.

'Mmm, it's delicious.'

'Good.'

Despite Amelia not showing any signs of deception, Melissa couldn't shake off the feeling that she had an agenda. For a moment, Melissa wondered if she was in cahoots with Vogue in an attempt to do some digging, then quickly brush that aside. It was Melissa who suggested Amelia come to her place, not the other way around. And it wasn't as if Amelia hadn't been out with her before. No, she was just being paranoid.

They finished their meal before moving into the living room, where they sat on the floor side by side, their wine glasses within reach on the coffee table.

'D'you want to talk about what happened between you and Cecile. You were really upset earlier,' Melissa said.

'Yeah, but I'm feeling better now. I've just got to accept that I can't change other people's behaviour, only my own.'

'I learnt that a long time ago.' Melissa leant across the table and picked up the remote control for the music centre. Seconds later, soft music filled the air.

'You say that like you've experienced crap relationships too.'

'You could say that.'

'Parents or friends?'

Melissa was on the verge of telling Amelia that she didn't want to talk about her past, when she suddenly had the urge to open up to her. There was something about Amelia that made her feel safe to talk to.

'I was adopted…' Melissa glanced over at Amelia who looked back at her with an open expression.

'I'm sorry, that must've been painful.'

'It was. Still is sometimes. It's the not knowing what you did wrong that hurts the most. The rejection.'

'I'm not trying to justify why someone would give their baby away, but in some circumstances, the mother might not be able to cope.'

'If that was the case, why would they then go on to have another child and keep her, it!'

'Circumstances change I suppose. Look, what I'm trying to say is that I don't think it's anything to do with the child per se. I mean, look at you, any woman would be proud to call you their daughter.'

Melissa had to fight back the tears as her body became awash with all the emotions she had suppressed for years. 'You don't need to say that.'

'It's true.'

Melissa's voice was full of emotion. 'Sue and Ted, my adoptive, you know... they had a picture of me when I was a baby, that's how I found her... they knew roughly where she was living at the time... and I got lucky.'

'Did you make contact?'

'I couldn't. She was ill but her... family didn't want the stress from the past to make her condition worse.'

'That's so sad.'

Melissa brushed away a single tear that rolled down her cheek with the back of her hand. 'I lost my last chance to meet her.' *Because Vogue stopped me.*

How many letters had she written to Vogue explaining who she was, only to be told that the police would be called if she made any attempt to approach any members of the family? When she had seen her mother's obituary in the newspaper the following week, she was heartbroken. She watched the family grieve from afar. Her mother was dead, and her half-sister was to her as well. Nothing on earth could make her forgive Vogue for denying her the opportunity to meet her own mother before she died.

'Have you still got the picture?'

'Yeah.'

'Can I see it?' Amelia said smiling. 'I'd love to see what you looked like as a baby.'

Melissa pushed herself onto her feet and went in search of the photo in her office, returning with it shortly after and sitting back down.

'Here you go,' Melissa said as she handed Amelia

the photo. 'Me and my mum.'

Amelia's eyes widened. 'She's… she's … beautiful…'

'She was,' Melissa said proudly. 'I wish I could've got to know her before she died.'

Amelia took a mouthful of wine, draining it in one go.

Melissa laughed. 'You trying to make yourself sick, knocking it back like that.'

'Sorry, I was um… thirsty.'

Melissa took the photo back from Amelia, leaving her fingers in contact with Amelia's for a little longer than required.

'You know,' Melissa leant forward and touched Amelia's cheek, 'you can always stay here if you don't want to go back to Cecile's tonight.'

Melissa saw the rise and fall of Amelia's chest.

'I… I can't. I don't want to make things worse with Cecile. She'll think I'm giving her the silent treatment or something.'

'Okay. Understood,' Melissa dropped her hand to her side quickly. 'D'you mind if we call it a night. I've got to be in the office early tomorrow.'

Melissa noticed the look of relief on Amelia's face and realised the truth had been staring at her the whole time. Amelia wasn't attracted to her. Probably never was. Their first meeting was an anomaly. Maybe there had been chemistry between them but there wasn't anymore.

They both got to their feet. 'Well, thanks for a lovely evening, Melissa.'

Amelia reached out and hugged her. Holding her tight.

This to Melissa was worth more than anything that could have happened in the bedroom. For the first time in her life, she felt visible. Connected to another human being.

Feeling an overwhelming sense of emotion wash over her, Melissa drew back. 'Let's do this again soon.'

'Definitely.'

Melissa walked her to the door, and they hugged briefly again. Shutting the door behind her, Melissa exhaled a deep breath.

How was she going to get over a woman she was slowly falling in love with? A woman who she knew would never love her back.

It felt like her mother's loss all over again.

Chapter Thirty-Four

The sound of the doorbell startled Vogue. She wasn't expecting anyone. She opened the front door and could do nothing but stare at the woman standing a few feet away from her. To say she was dumbstruck was an understatement. Vogue swallowed hard, finding it difficult to speak. She could hardly believe the woman in front of her had the gall to show her face.

Bev's eyes assessed Vogue.

'I had to come back, Vogue,' Bev said, taking a step towards her with a look of desperation on her face.

Was this why Bev had returned? To try and find redemption? If she had, she wasn't going to receive it from Vogue.

Her foot on the threshold, Vogue closed the door slightly, forcing Bev to step back.

'What do you want?'

'We need to talk, but not out here.'

'I'm not letting you in. Just say what you've got to say then leave.'

'Please, just five minutes. I promise, just let me have my say and I'll go. You won't ever have to see me again.'

'You say that like it's your choice.'

'I didn't mean it like that.'

Vogue hesitated for a moment as she tried to figure out what to do. Would letting her speak give Vogue the closure she needed to finally put Bev's betrayal behind her, or would it only make the wound deeper if her explanation wasn't plausible.

'Please, this is for your benefit as much as mine.'

Vogue pulled the door back to let her in and gestured for Bev to follow her to the living room.

Vogue stopped in the centre of the room, wrapping her arms around her chest to create a protective barrier.

'Well?'

'Vogue, I don't know where to start or how to explain all of this, but you need to know the truth about Melissa.'

Vogue frowned. 'Melissa? What the hell are you talking about?'

'She's behind all of this… she found out about me having an affair with John.'

'What! So not only are you a lying bitch, you're a cheat as well?'

'It wasn't sexual. It was emotional, but it didn't matter, she threatened to tell Ted unless I….'

'Unless you what?'

'Used those designs for the clothing line.'

Vogue burst out laughing, unable to stop herself.

'I didn't know they were plagiarized at the time. If I did, I never would've done it, but she said she was trying to help a friend gain confidence. That if she saw a company like Styles using them, she'd be more likely to grow. I know this sounds really stupid and naïve now, but I was at my wits' end.'

'You really think I'm going to buy this nonsense?'

Bev drew in a shaky breath. 'It doesn't matter if

you believe me or not. I had to warn you to be careful. Melissa has it in for you—'

'And why would that be?'

'I have no idea.'

'Just leave, Bev. I can't believe how low you've sunk, not that it should surprise me.'

'I understand you're angry. I fucked up big time. I know I should've come to you at the time, but I was ashamed of what I was doing.'

'I've heard enough. I want you to leave.'

'Please.' Bev's plea broke off and in those next few seconds, Vogue was done with hearing more of her lies.

'I said enough!' Vogue raised her voice, fighting back the tears she could feel prickling in the back of her eyes. She wouldn't show Bev that she was still upset, she'd rather die than let her see her shed one tear. 'Now get the fuck out of my house.'

It took Vogue a while to calm down after Bev left. She alternated between smashing something and wanting to lose herself in a bottle of wine.

How could she walk into Vogue's house and lie straight to her face?

Was it just a ploy to see her again? To witness the damage she had caused up close and personal. Well, Vogue wasn't going to give her the satisfaction. She wasn't going to be pushed out of the industry. She was going to leave. With her head held high.

The battle wasn't worth fighting.

Day after day, Vogue had tried, despite feeling as if she had the weight of the world on her shoulders, but she was tired. Mentally. Physically. Emotionally.

She had almost come to terms with the fact that her house would have to be sold to pay off her debts. As much as this crushed her, she knew she had to put the past behind her.

The house. Work. Even Amelia. This saddened her the most as she thought they might have a future together. One where they worked side by side, in a job they both had a passion for.

What the hell! She knew alcohol wasn't the answer, but she needed something to bring her down from the edge, and quick.

Just as she filled her glass to the rim, the doorbell sounded again. Vogue shook her head. *There was no way on earth that woman would be dense enough to come back.*

If it was her, Vogue wasn't going to be as restrained this time around. Swinging the door back with force, her words caught in her throat upon seeing Amelia.

'We need to talk.'

Amelia didn't wait to be invited in, she simply brushed past her and headed down the hallway, disappearing from view when she entered the kitchen.

Amelia was drinking Vogue's wine when she returned.

'Are you here to apologise?' Vogue asked.

'What? No – why should I? You both lied to me.'

'No, I didn't. I just assumed Cecile would've told you. Also, for your information, I am not working my way through the office.'

Amelia's cheeks flushed as she gulped the last of

the wine. 'Okay, I'm sorry. I shouldn't have said that.'

'So what's the matter?' Vogue said in response to her near empty glass.

'I think you'd better sit down.'

'You're not pregnant, are you?' Vogue said grinning.

'This isn't a joke.' Amelia poured another glass of wine which she handed to Vogue.

'Sounds serious.' Vogue took the glass, pulled out a chair and sat down.

Amelia kneeled in front of her. 'There's no other way to say this, so I'm just gonna say it. Melissa's your sister.'

Vogue stared at her blankly, unable to fully comprehend what Amelia had just said.

'Amelia, has that drink gone straight to your head?'

'No, it's true. She has a picture of your mum and she is holding a baby, but that baby isn't you. It's Melissa. She gave her up for adoption.'

'She told you it was my mum?'

'No, she never said a word about you. Vogue, I'd recognise your mum's eyes anywhere. And I swear, I'm not imagining things.'

It was Vogue's turn to down her drink this time. She remembered the letter received from a woman near the end of her mother's life. At the time, Vogue thought the woman was obviously mistaken, as her mother had never mentioned having another child. She had even gone as far as enquiring with each family member and they all assured her that her mother would never have been able to keep a secret like that. There wasn't any reason why she would have to. It wasn't as if her grandparents had been ogres. They loved her mother and would never have turned their back on her if she was pregnant.

But what if they were all wrong? What if she had been too quick to accept their word for it? Why hadn't she met her in person, if only to hear her side of the story.

Vogue knew why. She was grief stricken. Not in her full senses. But if it was true and Melissa was her sister, Vogue had denied her the one opportunity to meet her biological mother.

'I can't believe it.'

'I swear—'

'No, I believe you. I mean, I can't believe Melissa is… Bev came around earlier. She said Melissa set me up and I didn't believe her because I couldn't think what her motive would be. Guess I now know.'

'What're you going to do?'

'I think I need to talk to Bev.' Vogue stood. 'And there's no time like the present.'

Chapter Thirty-Five

Amelia sat in the cab next to Vogue, feeling as if she was in the twilight zone. From this morning's bombshell about Vogue and Cecile sleeping together, to now finding out that Melissa and Vogue were sisters. What could possibly happen next? The Prime Minister announcing contact had been made with aliens? To be honest, it wouldn't surprise her.

Amelia was stunned to think of the web of lies and deceit she had unassumingly walked into. All since arriving in London. Smoke and mirrors came to mind. No one was who they first portrayed themselves as, apart from Vogue. It seemed she was the only authentic person out of them all. The only one who hadn't lied.

And now they were going to face a woman Vogue had thought betrayed her, only to find out she hadn't. Not for the reasons she first thought anyway.

Amelia's temples pounded.

Just to think, this time last night I was wrapped up in Vogue's arms, having the time of my life.

Another twenty minutes of driving and the car finally came to a halt outside a row of similar looking houses.

Amelia thanked the driver and followed in Vogue's footsteps up a narrow path.

After pressing on the bell several times and getting no response, Vogue turned to Amelia in frustration.

'Great, she's not—'

'Vogue?'

Vogue and Amelia turned in the direction of the voice at the same time. Amelia stood back and watched as the woman, who she assumed was Bev, approached Vogue.

'I'm sorry I didn't believe you.' Vogue reached out and embraced Bev as she neared.

'So am I. So am I,' Bev sobbed as the two women held each other tightly. Amelia couldn't hear what they were saying but there seemed to be a lot of apologizing going on. When they finally parted, Bev led the way into her house.

Inside Bev's house, Amelia felt like a stranger looking in as the two caught up. Vogue and Amelia sat at the kitchen table while Bev put the kettle on. Had Amelia been a tad more confident, she would have asked for a large brandy from the bottle on the worktop.

'Sorry, I should have introduced you. Bev, this is Amelia, one of the trainees we recently hired.'

Amelia didn't miss Bev raising her eyebrows at Vogue in a 'Oh really' look.

'She's amazing,' Vogue said. 'Wait until you see her designs.'

'I'm sure she is,' Bev said and gave Amelia a warm genuine smile. 'Nice to meet you, Amelia. Just sorry it's under these circumstances.'

'Me too,' Amelia said, getting ready to tell her how much she admired her work, but decided now wasn't the time.

Bev went about getting mugs out of the cupboard

and dropping a spoonful of coffee in each of them.

'I came back to warn you. Once I read online that you were gearing up for a new collection, I knew Melissa would be up to her old tricks again.'

'This has all been such a shock, I can barely take it in,' Vogue said.

'Are you going to tell her you know?' Bev poured the hot water in the cups and added milk before placing a mug in front of them both.

'I don't think so. Not yet anyway.'

'So what're you going to do?' Bev took a seat at the table.

'I don't know. It's not every day you find out you have a sister.'

'An evil one at that,' Bev added.

'I don't think she's evil.' The words were out of Amelia's mouth before she could stop them.

The women turned towards her.

'Are you saying you think what Melissa did was okay?' Vogue asked.

It was one of those moments when Amelia wished the floor would swallow her whole. It was a bad habit of hers – engaging her mouth before her brain. Melissa had put both women through hell, yet here she was about to defend her.

'It's just that…' Amelia's voice was weak and high-pitched. She had to clear her throat in order to speak in a normal tone. 'I don't think any of this would have happened if it wasn't for the fact that she found out she was adopted. Look, I'm not saying I know Melissa that well, but I can tell you something, she is genuinely broken. Can you imagine people lying to you all your life, then one day the world you thought you knew turns upside down? Stupid question, of course you both do. So, if it was traumatic for you, imagine what it was like for Melissa then to find out her mother was dying. I'm sorry, Vogue, I realise in the whirlwind of your mother's illness, nothing but your mum mattered, but you had her in your life, while Melissa – she never got a chance to say hello or goodbye. Never got the chance to ask the questions only your mother could answer.'

'But that doesn't excuse what she did, Amelia,' Vogue said.

'Hurt people hurt people,' Amelia said softly. 'Thanks for the coffee but I'm gonna get going.'

'You don't have to go,' Vogue said.

'I do,' Amelia replied, 'You two look like you've got a lot to talk about.'

After saying their goodbyes, Amelia left. Standing outside on the pavement, she looked heavenwards and inhaled a deep breath. *If anyone's up there and you can hear me, please sort this mess out before it gets any worse.*

Taking her phone from her pocket, she tapped on the Uber app and was about to put her home address in when she had a change of heart. Something told her she needed to be somewhere else tonight.

Twenty minutes later, Amelia was in Melissa's flat on the sofa, Melissa's head resting on her lap.

'Thank you for coming back,' Melissa said, her words slurring.

'It's okay.' Amelia stroked the top of Melissa's head, feeling Melissa's tears soak through her trousers. 'Something told me you'd need a friend tonight.'

***

The following morning sat across the table from Melissa having breakfast, Amelia felt like Judas. Was she sitting with the enemy? While she totally sympathised with Melissa's plight, she couldn't help but feel she was betraying Vogue by being there. On the other hand, she felt like a bitch not forewarning Melissa about Vogue being in the know about their relationship.

'You're quiet this morning,' Melissa said, looking sheepish. 'I'm sorry about last night.'

'Hey, you've got nothing to apologise for. You were upset. There's no shame in that.'

'But crying….'

'D'you think I don't cry? Come on, Melissa, we're all human.'

'You're a really nice person, you know that?'

'You say it like you're surprised.'

'That's because I am. It's not every day you meet genuine people. Especially in this business.'

'Talking of business, have you decided what you're going to do?'

'Take off for a while. Clear my head. When I get back, who knows?'

'If you don't want to talk about this just tell me to mind my own business, but do you think it's worth trying to get in touch with your sister again?'

'Never! And you're spot on. I don't want to talk about it.' Melissa rose to her feet and took her dishes to the sink. 'That part of my life is well and truly over.'

'It just seems so sad that you're both missing out on getting to know one another.'

'Trust me, I'm not missing out on anything.'

Amelia wished she could talk about the positives of Melissa's relationship with Vogue. Together they had built something great – a feat neither could have achieved without the other. They were stronger together but just didn't know it. But she wouldn't say anything. She was becoming quite apt at being the good liar herself. The one who could hide words behind a veil. Who knew what she'd be in a year's time? A politician?

'I just thought I'd throw it out there. You know how you feel.'

'Yes, I do,' Melissa cast a glance over her shoulder, 'and it's far from sisterly love.'

'Suppose I'd better go home and change for work. That's if I've still got a job or a roof over my head for that matter.'

Cecile had been messaging her, but Amelia couldn't find the right moment to reply, and even if she did, there really wasn't much to say. But it was another thing she had to straighten out. She couldn't leave things the way they were.

Melissa dried her hands on the kitchen towel as she turned to face her. 'You know you can stay here. I don't know how long I'll be gone but you can flat sit.'

'No, I couldn't,' Amelia said, feeling even worse at her generosity.

'What's your other choice? Go back to Bournemouth? I'm not being mean but there aren't many opportunities up there for you. You need to be in London where everything's happening. You know what they say about looking a gift horse in the mouth.'

'I'm not. I'm just trying to say... I don't think you should leave. Not until you sort things out with your sister.'

'And I've told you, there's nothing to sort out,' Melissa said with finality. 'I'm not contacting her again

'Okay, thanks for the offer. I don't know what I'm going to do either. I'll just have to play it by ear for now.'

That went for everything. Except when it came down to Vogue.

She hoped that part of her life was now sorted.

Chapter Thirty-Six

Alone in her flat, Melissa stared at the empty seat that had been filled by Amelia moments earlier. Her words still doing their rounds in her mind – reconcile with Vogue, forgive her. In all the months that had passed, she had never once even considered such an idea. After all, Vogue had rejected her at the outset, why would she change her mind now? Especially if she found out it was Melissa, after all of this time playing her side kick. All of the lies.

What was she doing even giving Amelia's words any weight? Amelia didn't understand what she'd been through. And yet, in that moment, it came to her clearly. What had Melissa actually achieved in all this time feeling bitter, plotting for the right moment to strike?

Nothing. That's what. A big fat zero.

When Melissa compared it to what she'd lost, she realised it was everything. Most importantly, she'd lost herself in the process of trying to get even in a fight with another person who didn't even know one was taking place.

This had to stop. Since she was the one who'd started it, it was up to her to put an end to it once and for all, and to hell with the consequences.

Melissa picked up the phone and called Tina.

An hour later, Melissa had rehearsed what she would say to Vogue several times in her head until her words were on autoplay. She knew Vogue would try and change her mind and make her stay, but she couldn't. They needed to part ways for both their sakes.

'Whoooo hooooo,' was the first thing Melissa heard as she stepped out of the lift on the third floor.

People were running around hollering, giving each other high fives in victory.

'Hey, Melissa, great news eh?' Claire came running towards her and grabbed Melissa in a tight bear hug. 'Can you believe it?'

Before Melissa had a chance to utter a response, Claire took off to find another body to hug.

'Melissa, Vogue said to go straight to her office when you got here,' Carol said as she made her way down the corridor towards her office.

Melissa told herself not to panic. It wasn't an unusual request; it was her sheer paranoia making her overthink. *Just be normal.*

She tapped on Vogue's open door and walked in. 'You wanted to see me?'

Vogue looked up at her from her desk and Melissa knew immediately that something had changed. She could just feel it in the air.

'Yes.'

Melissa went to take a seat, but Vogue stood.

'Don't sit,' Vogue said, putting her jacket on. 'We need to talk.'

'Okay. Sounds serious. Am I being fired?' Melissa said, trying to make light of her comment.

Vogue ignored her question and headed for the door. 'Let's go.'

'Where're we going?' Melissa asked, following Vogue down the corridor towards the lift.

By now her nerves were on edge. If Vogue knew something, she'd rather just get it out in the open instead of prolonging her misery.

Vogue's answer was curt and to the point. 'For a drive.'

'That doesn't tell me much. Where exactly?'

'You'll see.'

This wasn't good. Melissa couldn't sense any anger from Vogue. In fact, she couldn't sense anything but an urgency to get going, wherever that was to.

Vogue only spoke once they were in the car and on their way to north London.

'I take it you've heard Tina is back on board with us?'

'I didn't actually, but I just assumed that was the case by the good mood everyone's in.'

'Don't you think it's strange that she changed her mind at the last minute?'

'Not really. Amelia's designs are amazing. She'd have been stupid not to use them.'

Melissa looked out of the window as they passed a signpost signalling they were on their way to Southgate.

'So are you looking forward to the mayhem that's about to follow? It'll be just like the old days.'

'About that, Vogue. I was thinking. I need a break from things for a while.'

'Oh.' Vogue kept her eyes on the road.

'Yeah,' Melissa said, trying to sound casual. 'I've

decided to go travelling.'

'When did you decide this?'

'It's been on my mind for some time.'

Vogue slowed the car as they went downhill.

'You don't need me anyway,' Melissa said. Saying that made her feel sad. 'You can manage on your own.'

'That's not true. I've always thought of us as a team.'

'That's never been the case, let's be honest.' Tears prickled Melissa's eyes. 'I've always been your underdog.'

Vogue glanced at her briefly. 'Is that what you really think?'

'It's what I know.'

'I'm sorry you felt that way. And I'm sorry for the way I've treated you. But I want you to know I couldn't have done any of this without you, and neither would I have wanted to.'

Melissa had been so busy listening to Vogue that she hadn't realised that they'd turned into Southgate cemetery.

'What're we doing here?' Melissa asked, looking out of the window at all the gravestones lined up next to one another.

'I told you I want to talk.'

'We could have gone to a café for that.'

Vogue pulled her car over to the kerb, turned off the engine and climbed out without saying a word. After a few seconds of wondering whether to run, Melissa joined her as she weaved her way in and out of the large section of graves.

When she finally caught up with her, Vogue was standing in front of her mother's grave. Their mother's grave.

A lump formed in her throat as she resisted the urge to drop to her knees and cradle the headstone. Her mother's remains were there but her soul wasn't. She would never know what it would have been like to be held in her arms. To be reassured that everything was going to be all right.

Melissa couldn't even openly grieve because she was a secret. No one would ever know that Mavis wasn't the mother of only one child but two.

An involuntary sob left her throat and she quickly moved to try and cover her mouth. But her hand was stopped by Vogue who took hold of it and held it in her own.

Looking down at the grave, Vogue said, her voice full of emotion. 'Mum, I'd like to introduce you to your daughter Heather.'

Melissa gasped. 'How d'you know my name?'

'I did a background search on you. Something I should have done when you first sent your letter.' She turned to her. 'I am so sorry, Heather.'

It was strange hearing Vogue call her by her real name.

'How long have you known?'

'Not very long. But none of that matters now. I want to make it up to you the best I can.'

Footsteps and voices came from behind and she frowned when she saw Amelia and a workman heading in their direction.

'Here we are,' Amelia said.

'Right, the workman said, bending down on his knees in front of the gravestone. 'So you want to add another name on here?'

'Yes. Survived by her daughters Vogue Willis and Heather Lynne.'

Vogue laughed. 'Why are you looking up there, Amelia?'

'Oh,' Amelia smiled. 'I'm just saying a big thank you!'

Chapter Thirty-Seven

Amelia rolled away from Vogue onto her back, her body slick with sweat after the mammoth sex session. She could barely catch her breath, but Vogue looked like it had been a stroll in the park for her.

'How're you not knackered? We've being going at it for hours.'

Vogue turned to face her smiling. 'Because I have zero stress on my mind. The business is doing great and I'm solvent again. I still own my house and my best friend is back in my life. What more could I ask for?'

Amelia narrowed her eyes. 'Ahem.'

'What?' Vogue feigned innocence. 'Have you got a dry mouth? D'you want some water?'

Amelia twisted her lips to the side and rolled her eyes.

Vogue laughed as she pulled Amelia into her arms. 'And most importantly I've got you.'

'You're lucky you said that,' Amelia said, joining in with her laughter.

'Oh yeah and why's that?'

Amelia lifted the quilt revealing her naked body. 'Because you wouldn't have been getting any more of that.'

'Does that mean—'

'No!' Amelia playfully slapped away Vogue's roaming hands. 'Later. We really should've started dinner by now, Melissa will be here soon.'

'Why are you torturing me?' Vogue said, exhaling a frustrated breath.

Amelia widened her eyes. 'Vogue you can't possibly want to do it again. I can barely feel myself down there. I've had so many orgasms, I think I'd make it into the Guinness book of records.'

'Are you complaining?'

'No way, but she just needs a little time to adjust to all the activity.'

They'd been seeing each other exclusively for eight months now and Amelia's sex life had gone from a drought to an oasis. Her vagina didn't know what was happening.

'You're so beautiful,' Vogue suddenly said, tracing Amelia's jawline with the tip of her finger.

'Are you trying to sweet talk me?'

'No, I'm trying to tell you that… I love you.'

Amelia blinked rapidly, not sure how to respond. She'd been praying for this moment for months, and now Vogue had said it without any prompting, she felt exactly how she imagined she would be – ecstatically happy.

'And I love you too,' Amelia said blinking away tears of happiness.

'D'you think we should—'

Amelia laughed as she quickly rolled over and leapt out of bed. 'You're so naughty. Come on, I'll let you take a shower with me if you promise to be good.'

Vogue gave her a mischievous grin as she climbed out of bed to join her.

An hour later, after giving in to a quick sex session in the shower, Amelia sat opposite Vogue, Melissa and Bev.

Although Melissa's actions weren't completely forgiven, the three women were still working on rebuilding broken connections by taking things day by day. Amelia was glad to see they were getting there.

'I never thought I'd see this day,' Bev said. 'All of us sitting here together.'

'Me neither and I swear I will never stop trying to make it up to you both,' Melissa said.

'You don't have to,' Vogue said taking hold of her hand. 'I take ownership in the part I played in all of this.'

Vogue lifted her wine glass.

'I'd like to make a toast. To family, friendship, and…' Vogue stared fondly at each of the women, 'unconditional love.'

The three women followed suit and raised their glasses.

'I'll drink to that!' Amelia said, tilting her glass first in Vogue's direction, then heavenwards, silently thanking the Universe for answering her prayer.

Vogue laughed. 'Have you got an invisible friend, Amelia?'

'You could say that.' Amelia smiled. 'I'm just thanking them for receiving much, much more than I asked for!'

If Amelia doubted it before, she didn't anymore. There was a greater force at work that was unseen.

All it took was to let go of resistance and leave the rest in fate's hands.

ABOUT THE AUTHOR

Based in Dorset, UK, Jade Winters is a passionate author with a particular focus on lesbian fiction. Jade always enjoys discussing her books with readers. You can connect with her by visiting her website at www.jade-winters.com or get in touch with her via Facebook or Instagram.

Printed in Great Britain
by Amazon